Bertha De Jongh

Loving and Loth

A novel

Bertha De Jongh

Loving and Loth
A novel

ISBN/EAN: 9783337052447

Printed in Europe, USA, Canada, Australia, Japan

Cover: Foto ©Andreas Hilbeck / pixelio.de

More available books at **www.hansebooks.com**

LOVING AND LOTH.

A Novel.

BY THE AUTHOR OF

"ROSA NOEL" AND "THE SISTERS LAWLESS."

> " Escape me?
>   Never——
>   Beloved!
>   While I am I, and you are you,
>   So long as the world contains us both,
>   Me the loving, and you the loth,
>   While the one eludes
>   Must the other pursue . . . ."
>   R. BROWNING.

IN THREE VOLUMES.
VOL. I.

LONDON:

RICHARD BENTLEY AND SON.

1875.

CONTENTS TO VOL I.

LOVING AND LOTH.

CHAPTER I.

THEIR NEAREST NEIGHBOUR.

DOWN in the heart of the slumberous country, away from the railway and from society, lived Susie and her mother.

Susie, being pale and plain, and without the charm of fortune, bade fair to be one of the shabbily-served many for whom no lover has ever sighed, and whom no suitor has wooed.

Susie knew her short-comings. Already she had begun to learn that she was ugly and unpleasing, and it gave her a heart-ache; for if she had not a longing to be loved, she longed mightily to enjoy life—to have it, indeed, one long pastime.

Feeling herself an inadequate cause to produce any wished-for effect, she aimed at having brighter fortunes brought to her by the person she loved best in the world—her mother.

Mrs. Dawnay had been married from the school-room, widowed while yet in her teens, and now at four-and-thirty was still beautiful and redolent of youth.

Susie, with her light gray eyes, pale skin, and little humorous turned-up nose, might have been any age from twelve to thirty. She was in reality seventeen; but for the promotion of her interests she wore her hair hanging down her back in a curly mass, her dresses to her ankles, and personated with ease not quite fifteen. She knew herself to be thought and spoken of as an ugly little girl with disagreeable manners. Her mother's admirers shirked her, the very servants pronounced it to be a pity that she had not beautiful fair hair, and a pretty complexion, and a taking way with her, like her mamma.

The lovely widow and her ugly daughter had roamed about on the Continent till they were tired of it. They had done Ems and Spa, and Biarritz, Nice and Cannes, and Mentone, in a cheap, unsatisfactory sort of way ; and with a loathing of foreign places and manners upon them, and a longing in their hearts for peace and repose, crossed the Channel, strayed through England, and finally nestled themselves down in the little home [that had been left Mrs.

Dawnay by her dead mother. It was lonely, quaint, and rustic. They suffered whimsical tortures at first from terror of burglars, earwigs, and horned cattle; they exhausted the novel enjoyments of their own cow, their culinary experiments in their own kitchen, their pedestrian experiments of wandering off, and getting lost in lonely lanes.

Then came a weariness of this dull life; a sense of miss and loss after the thorny pleasures of other days. But this, too, passed; the current of their life flowed on evenly, if a little sluggishly. They had no events to mark the days with; monotonous and neutral-tinted, the hours succeeded each other. They got to know a few people about them; that is to say, they had a formal acquaintance with them: all but one.

Dear to Susie's heart was their nearest neighbour, whose old home, rich in romantic tradition and memory of the past, hid itself behind ivy-clasped trees, only showing a blood-shot eye on winter evenings, when the leaves had grown few, and the sun was glowing red in the west.

Sir Alfred Ogle was an estimable, courteous, rather diffident old gentleman, who had a way of beginning fine and long-worded sentences, and then not being able to finish them to his own satisfaction or that of his hearer, limping off discreditably in little common-place words that left bare the little common-place idea of the whole speech.

He was unmarried, and was without any heir of his name to his large property, which, being unentailed, was presumably to fall to a fortunate young relative on the mother's side.

" Let us go and gather wild roses, Mèry, and have the room filled with them to-morrow when Sir Alfred comes," said Susie to her mother one day in July.

" *Wild* roses !" repeated Mrs. Dawnay, turning her large liquid eyes and fixing them on her daughter's frank gray ones; " why, the hedges are full of them, Susie."

" I know they are ; and see if Sir Alfred does not think it *sad* for us to have nothing but wild roses ; he will send us over a quantity of tame ones, I am sure he will ; his gardens are crowded with them."

" I do not care for his roses, do you, Susie ?"

" I care for anything that is his, which finds its way over as a friendly offering to us"—(Susie was always delicately careful to enshroud her schemes in ambiguity).— " Sir Alfred will come in here to-morrow," she went on, "and he will say, 'How charmingly you have adorned your drawing-room with the unassuming product of— the hedges.' Then I will say childishly, 'I made Mèry go with me.' Then he will say sentimentally, 'What! you insisted on your mamma's subjecting herself unnecessarily to the ardours of—old Sol?' Come, mother, put on that hat of yours so simple, yet so serious; make up your mind that sheep are harmless; try and think of them, if we meet them, as simply mutton, and let us go now; it is nearly half-past four."

Susie jumped off the window-sill, where she had been sitting, and went upstairs to her room, as she finished speaking.

The following day, when Sir Alfred Ogle came to luncheon, he entered a room crowded with pale and dying humble relations of the Queen of Flowers.

He came in exceedingly warm, and pain-
fully, embarrassedly conscious of the fact.
He seemed to see nothing *sad* in the idea
of the widow decking her little drawing-
room with eglantine; and though many of
his remarks were flowery enough, they had
no sort of reference to his own roses.

Susie he treated as usual, as something
much less than woman, and rather more
than child. She went to sleep in her low
wicker chair soon after lunch, just in the
midst of a story he was telling, and he
felt more inclined to think of her as a child
than he had ever done before.

He and the widow, sitting on either side
the open window, with a little breeze blowing refreshingly over them, discovered that
they had many coincidences of opinion and
taste, but somehow Mrs. Dawnay found
time to remember that the room was warm,

the minutes not winged, the luncheon and profound quiet narcotic, and that Susie was asleep.

It was the very last day of July.

"On Tuesday I expect my nephew—my nephew on the distaff side. He comes on board his yacht to Cowes, and usually stays with me until the commencement of the gaieties of the regatta week, when he carries me off with him."

"Oh!" said Susie, suddenly; so suddenly that they almost started. "Then you are going away from St. Quentin's?"

"For an inconsiderable time. Yes," he answered, looking at her with 'a smile; "I remain with Eugene until the seasons of nautical festivity are concluded in all the places where they have regatta weeks; pigs, poles, and all that sort of thing, you know."

"Oh," said Susie again, in a relieved tone, " then you will soon be back. You are such a nice neighbour, we should be sorry to lose you."

This with the allowable ingenuousness and simplicity of not quite fifteen.

Sir Alfred uncrossed his legs, and re-crossed them. Perhaps he would have blushed a little, if the warmth of the room had not given his face all the colour of which it was susceptible.

Mrs. Dawnay, fanning herself gently with a black fan whereon Susie had painted will-o'-the-wisps with lamps, looked at her daughter meanwhile. How ugly she was ! even her partial mother's eyes could see no beauty, nor faint approach to beauty, in that pertest of snub noses, those most honest of green-gray eyes, that little mouth turning up waggishly at the corners, that colourless skin.

The widow moved slightly, and so caught the reflection of her own oval face with its apple-blossom tint, and crowned by ropes of waving golden hair. She sighed, and twisted her head impatiently away. Why could not Susie have inherited some of that waning loveliness she had just seen?

Sir Alfred caught the sigh; it seemed to him a fitting sequel to Susie's little speech.

Susie went on with her catechism. "Is your nephew married?"

"My nephew is not yet in matrimonial fetters,—no. He is an admirable representative of the jeunesse dorée of the period. He is a young man about town: good-tempered; fair; good features; blue eyes, and all the rest of it."

"Ugh!" said Susie, with a pronounced shudder; "we always wish to have averted from us the youth of the period, don't we mamma? We don't like these sprigs with their fair hair and blue eyes, do we?"

Mrs. Dawnay smiled slightly, and closing her fan, leaned one soft pink cheek on it, her elbow resting on her knee, her eyes roving over the basking fields and cool, dark copses, to the narrow strip of deeply blue water that lay against the paler sky.

Sir Alfred took a good long look at her, full of approval and admiration. Well, no one could accuse *him* of being a sprig with fair hair and blue eyes, for whatever tint his hair had been was now one of the concerns of the past. As for his eyes, they were the colour of medlars, and reminded one of those fruits of the earth.

"I think that my nephew will meet with

your approbation," he said. "He usually meets with the most unqualified admiration. He is a great favourite with ladies."

"Is he?" responded Mrs. Dawnay, with a dreamy gentleness; "I like pretty boys." Susie darted a look at her which caused her to qualify her speech by adding, "Or rather, I used so to do when I was younger than I am now. I have not the patience now that I then had, I fear, with their boyish over-estimation of themselves, their foolish little affectations, their transparent devices to appear older than they really are, their airy scepticism regarding things that they have not themselves yet proved or experienced, or that they have not yet learned to prize as truths."

"I agree with you," said Sir Alfred; "indeed, I discover many concurrences of opinion between yourself and me. We jump together, Mrs. Dawnay."

"We do agree in many things I think," answered the widow, with her gentle smile. "But what are you speaking of now? Not having patience with the foolishnesses and crudities of very young men, or in admitting that they are sometimes both foolish and crude?"

"Yes, exactly," rejoined Sir Alfred; "the latter." And he became absorbed in watching the strengthened breeze ruffling her smooth golden hair.

A few more little speeches, a few more smiles, and he rose to go. Outside the green garden gate a dog-cart was going up and down, waiting for him. The horses were superb, the servant and cart faultless. If everything belonging to him had not been perfect of its kind, he would have had some difficulty in getting rid of twelve thousand a year.

"You have no flower in your coat," said Susie, standing in front of him, and looking up at him with a boyish frankness. "*We* have nothing in the shape of a flower to offer you but a brier rose. You know we don't allow flowers in our garden; we grow all our own vegetables—every one. We have not a flower; all crowded out by the vegetable family. That is my doing; Mèry tried hard to keep one small corner, but one morning I got up with the early worm and pulled up all her flowers (they were half dead already, poor things, so that it did not matter); and by noon young Thomas and I had it planted with beans."

"Mary?" said Sir Alfred, in a sternly interrogative tone, and ignoring all the rest of her sentence. "Mary?"

"Don't think that when I call my mother Mèry, I call her M-a-r-y. That would be disrespectful ; besides, it isn't her name ; her name is Margaret. I call her M-è-r-y, patois, you know, for little mother."

"No," said Sir Alfred, "I must confess to ignorance. Thank you for your kind offer of a rose, Miss Susie, but I have over-stepped that period when to florally deco-rate affords any satisfaction. I never care to stick flowers in my coat now."

Then Sir Alfred went, and Susie rushed to the window to see him get into the dog-cart.

"Don't, Susie, it will embarrass him to feel that he is being watched. He cannot be very agile any longer, poor old fellow."

"That isn't *my* fault," said Susie, and kept her place.

Certainly his joints were not as limber

as they probably were twenty years before. Susie waited until she saw his harness flash in the full sunshine far up the road; then, crossing the room to where her mother now was, she seated herself on a footstool in front of her, and leaning her elbows on her knees, and resting both white cheeks on her hands until they were pressed upwards into giving her eyes an unnaturally crafty, foxy expression, gazed up at Mrs. Dawnay's face, and after a little silence spoke, and with energy.

" So many men have snubbed me, I should like just once to snub some man—I long to do it. Do you think this youth, this coming nephew, will be *snubbable,* mamma ?"

" No ; and I do not like to hear my daughter make such an acid speech as that. If you have been snubbed it is because you have seemed to be a sharp, disagreeable little girl. Why do you not plait or coil that long, rough mane? You would look older then."

"Thank you, mamma, but I had rather look fifteen than seventeen, and I should think you would rather have me; and about being snubbed, that is not the reason. If I had been a lovely little girl with golden hair and pink cheeks, no one would have had the heart to snub me. Have I not seen how nice your men friends could be to *pretty* little girls? No, I am not winsome. I once overheard Mr. McCheyne saying so to deaf Mr. Abbot. People are never drawn to me. They cannot be agreeable to me, and so they are disagreeable. I don't care!"

"Do not care, my Susie—you are too sensible to care. You are far cleverer than many of the men who, you say, snub you."

"What is the use of being clever if people don't like one?" said Susie, gloomily.

"Be cleverer still, Susie, and make them like you."

"How?"

"For one thing, never tell a story to match, as I have sometimes heard you. When a man tells a rather funny story, do not cap it by one of your own on the same theme, but funnier still; that is sure to annoy him. And you must be a better listener than you are now, to be agreeable. Remember how interesting the talker is to himself, and how it wounds self-love and pricks pride to see roving eyes, and a fidgety waiting for him to finish that you may begin talking yourself. Flattery is a weapon too coarse and clumsy for you ever to use ; but if you have a kind and gentle heart, out of its abundance you will give the sweetest, most acceptable flattery—that is spontaneous, that cannot be defined, that is delicate and intangible, yet delightful, and surely perceptible as the perfume of a violet. But after all, my child, I could talk to you till the sun rose again, and use all the words in the dictionary, yet I could not tell you how to make people like you. Perhaps the safest and shortest thing that I can say to you is—like people."

"I can't," said Susie, sighing ; "I don't feel drawn to them."

"Then they will never like you," rejoined Mrs. Dawnay, with decision.

"I would give—not my soul, exactly, but almost—to be unspeakably lovely, and to ride over men rough shod," said Susie, with a monotonous intensity.

" I am glad, then, that beauty has not been given you."

Susie flushed with wounded vanity.

"Always a dangerous gift, it would have been a fatal one to you, if a domineering and insatiable vanity had accompanied it."

Susie withdrew her elbows from her mother's lap, and, rising, walked bareheaded out of the house, and Mrs. Dawnay watched her promenading about on the grass in front of the windows, her thumbs stuck in her leather belt, and with a very cross face.

Tall and lithe, she moved hither and thither with a swift, careless grace. The now slanting sunbeams warmed her brown hair into dull gold here and there; her little irregular profile looked as if cut out of ivory, against the dark polished green of the laurels. A fox terrier that had been given to herself came out, and with canine persistency dogged her footsteps.

Her mother watched her sadly. She knew her to be proud and sensitive, suspicious and imaginative, luxury loving, and poverty hating; she knew her to have a longing for the beauty she could never possess, aspirations that would never be realized, hopes and wishes never to be gratified; in fact, she knew her to be handsomely dowered with every moral and mental attribute calculated to give her a most unhappy future.

Taking a low, light chair, the widow placed it outside the long window on the grass, and seated herself.

Presently Susie came running up to her, saying eagerly,

"He might yawn in my face, you know; men often do; it is a way they have, not only with me, but with others; then I could say, to snub him——"

"Say to whom?" asked Mrs. Dawnay.

"Why, the coming nephew," answered Susie, looking rather foolish.

"You may never see him, my dear; I do not know any reason to suppose that you should."

"Oh, no, of course not," said Susie, trying to look as if that idea had presented itself to her before; "but in time of peace prepare for war, you know."

Mrs. Dawnay only smiled, without answering. Her daughter, with a return of the huffed, injured look, to her face, darted away, and going to the back of the house, began working energetically in the garden. They did not meet again until dinner, and then Susie chatted as gaily as ever about a thousand nothings, that sounded spicy enough in her crisp and rapid utterance of them.

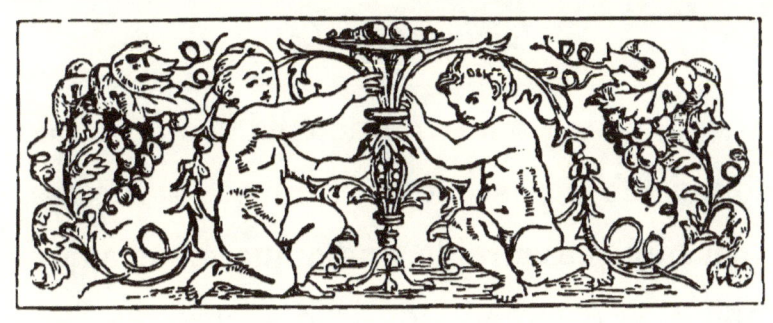

CHAPTER II.

"WITH VARIAND LOOK, RICHT LIKE A LORD UNSTABLE."

ON Tuesday, the 2nd of August, the fine iron gates of St. Quentin's swung open; a phaeton, with a pair of clean-pasterned, quaintly-clipped cobs, dashed through; a young man driving them gave a smile as sweet, brief, and bright as a coquette's, to the woman at the Lodge.

Sir Alfred's nephew had arrived.   He

was a young man who looked as if he had
found life a pastime, and himself a success,
pleasure pleasurable, and amusement enjoyable ; as if submission to disagreeable facts
had never been required of him, or anything in the shape of a dark foreboding
ever been present with him.

His uncle shook him warmly by the
hand, and said he was glad to see him,
glancing over his shoulder meanwhile at
the clock, that pointed to a quarter before
the dinner hour.

"Dinner in a quarter of an hour," said
he, and keeping his hand on his nephew's
shoulder, where he had placed it, walked
him gently out of the room and upstairs,
telling him as they went along that he
need not ask how he was, since he looked
as blooming as a young dog-rose. This
feeble fun required a laugh ; then Eugene

shut his uncle's laugh out, and his own in, and began preparing for dinner.

What a cook Sir Alfred had, and what wines, and what silver, and what turquoise-studded Sèvres!

"I am in love with this pouting, powdered beauty; I always have been," said Eugene, gazing amorously into his plate at dessert, and hesitating an instant before cutting an apricot on the charming face.

Sir Alfred, sitting sideways at the table, with his napkin tucked in at his neck like a bib, was gobbling grapes as if he were making his meal off them, and had not already fared sumptuously. He did not answer at once, for the best of reasons, and when he spoke, it was with a gigantic frog in his throat, that reduced his voice to a husky and mysterious whisper.

"Porcelain representations of the beguiling fair sex are the safest for boys to fall in love with. Give me the claret, Eugene, and, by the way, remind me not to forget to send or take some of these grapes to Mrs. Dawnay to-morrow."

" And who may Mrs. Dawnay be ?"

" I'll take you over and show you to-morrow ; she is worth seeing,"—with a shade of conviviality in his manner—" yes, by Gad ! she is the sort of woman to exhibit as a specimen, my neighbour, Mrs. Dawnay ; she really is."

" I am glad to hear it," replied Eugene, " as I am to have the advantage of seeing her to-morrow. And how about Mr. Dawnay ? Is he shadow or substance ? Is he food for the fishes ? the worms ? or the lovely Mrs. Dawnay ? Is he here or "—vaguely—" there ?"

" He has been dead these fifteen years."

" A widow ?"

" Yes, a widow," assented Sir Alfred, fidgeting, and helping himself again to claret.

" Good-bye St. Quentin's," said Eugene to himself. " A specimen widow in the heart of the country, a neighbour, and no one to protect him. Poor Uncle Ogle !"

" And is she lone and lorn ?" he said. " Does she live alone at—wherever she does live ?"

" No ; she has one little girl."

" And how high is the little girl; as high as the table ?"

" She is very nearly as tall as yourself," answered Sir Alfred, combating his nephew's flippant tone with a dignified one.

Eugene gave a slight exclamation.

" Grown up, eh ? Then the widow is no longer young, of course."

" She is not a day over five-and-thirty.

Her daughter cannot be more than fifteen. Are you ready for a cup of coffee, Eugene ?"

Eugene tried to lead him gently back to the subject that he had abruptly quitted, with intention ; but his uncle would not be led.

After coffee, Eugene smoked, and Sir Alfred slept. Outside, the moonlight flooded the park. The trees looked as if they could never rock and sigh and toss bare branches again ; they stood so leafy, so silent, and so motionless ; every little twig seemed sound asleep and dreaming, not a leaf stirred.

Eugene stepped softly out of the window on to the terrace, and stood bathed in moonlight, gazing out and up, by turns ; out on the cold and silvered and silent beauty of the earth ; up to heaven, where one or two restless stars shot past the tranquil moon, and their changeless sister stars, and fell into the abyss of space and were lost.

Eugene was not impressed by the scene. His heart felt as light as a wreath of his cigar smoke, his mind was full of petty plans (they did not seem petty to him) for the next few weeks : people whom he wanted on board his yacht, people whom he did not want ; this, that, and the other. Presently he began sauntering up and down on the broad, smooth stones, treading more on his toes than his heels, out of considerateness, as he passed the open windows of the dining-room. With a start and a grunt, Sir Alfred awoke just when the clock was finishing striking eleven. He came out and yawned in the moon's white face, gave a careless glance at the

idealization of his park, said " Good-night"
to Eugene, and went up to bed.   In a few
minutes his nephew followed him.

When the uncle and nephew made their
appearance at The Cottage the following
day, they found Mrs. Dawnay seated at
the piano singing, while Susie, her elbows
on her knees, her cheeks pressed upwards
into her eyes, was poring with knitted
brows over various scraps of paper—evidently bills and tradesmens' books—their
tradesmen came from Newport.

Mrs. Dawnay rose with her sweet and
winning grace, came forward, and shook
hands.   Susie rose too, turning her back
full on them for a moment, as she stuffed
the bills and books under the cushion of
her chair.

Sir Alfred introduced his nephew, Mr.
Everard.   " I have driven you over some

grapes, Mrs. Dawnay," he then said, trying to make his words sound as joke-like as possible.

" Thank you very much," answered the widow.

And " Thanks" came from Susie. " I adore grapes !"

" Does Sir Alfred call *this* a slip of a fellow ?" she was thinking as she glanced sideways at Eugene's hale, straight-featured face, with the eyes purely, clearly blue, that are rarely seen—burning blue eyes, full of light and life—and at his strongly-made figure. Then she thought what a guy she looked herself, in her draggled green percale, with its great round white spots like wafers. Her nervous fingers flew involuntarily to her hair, and it seemed to her that almost a yard away from her head she felt it bristling out rough and untidy. But she need not have troubled herself, Eugene was not observing her. She appeared to him to be an ugly little school-girl, only to be overlooked, not to be looked at.

Presently, however, he found that unless he talked to her he should be reduced to absolute silence, for his uncle had gone out at the French window with the widow, and was monopolizing her in the shade of a tall laurel, where each had taken a garden-chair.

He turned to Susie, who, feeling that she was not even looking a *neat* fright, averted her head with awkward shyness, giving him only her little pale snub-nosed profile to gaze at as he talked.

" Do you like Beaucombe, Miss Dawnay?"

" No, not much."

" It is too quiet for you, I suppose."

" How did you know that we had lived

on the Continent?" said Susie, turning her
eye out at him sideways like a vicious colt,
but not moving her head an inch.

"I did not know it," replied Eugene,
astounded.

"I thought from your saying that about
it's being too quiet for me, that of course
you had heard we had lived chiefly on the
Continent."

"No, I had never heard it. And you
like the Continent?"

"I like it about as well as I do Beaucombe."

"From your tone I should think that
you meant to say you hated both," said
Eugene, laughing.

"I do not hate either. I loved it here
until everything got to be so threadbare :
milking the cow, going primrosing, listening to the nightingales, going out into the

3—2

kitchen and making things that sounded delicious in a book——"

"But were not so delicious when they came to the table," supplied Eugene, as she paused. "Then you are tired of a country life?"

"Yes; *heart* of the country life, in a cottage. The country must be nice with horses, and a large place near a large town, and people full of news visiting you."

"But you have some pleasant neighbours about you here?"

"Only one or two, and they are all old."

"Oh, it is a bore for you if you have no little girls of your own age. You must be very lonely."

"Mamma is pretty nearly my own age," said Susie, calmly. "We like the same things usually too, and have fine quarrels, and makings up. It is just like having a sister."

"What a piquant and delightful state of affairs !"

Here the widow managed to get back into the room again, Sir Alfred close behind her. Eugene turned away from Susie with an air of relief that did not go unobserved, and addressed himself to Mrs. Dawnay.

"This is the most picturesque, jolly little spot," he said ; "I have often admired it in passing. I am very glad that it is inhabited at last."

"We like it very much. Almost the only drawback is, that Susie has no advantages, as she has no governess. It would be a great boon to be nearer town, where she could have masters."

Eugene murmured that it was a pity.

"However," said the widow, with a

bright smile, "we study together sometimes, she and I.   We improve our minds
with the least dry history we can find, and
translate French romance together."

Then Sir Alfred claiming her ear, she was
obliged to turn away, and Eugene to take
up with Susie again.

"Do you like French?"   Asking simple
questions was his only idea of conversation
with school-girls, particularly if they happened to be plain-featured.

"So that you need not be troubled to
find out any more of my likes and dislikes,
let me tell you that the only things I posi-
tively dislike are snobs and Satan."

Eugene saw the pretty mother's cheek
flush, although she was listening to Sir
Alfred with apparent interest and attention.   Susie certainly did not do credit to
her training.

"At all events," he answered, "that gentleman you mention is not a snob; he is a Prince, and a gentleman; and I confess to a sanguinary and snobbish weakness for *blood*," he added, a mischievous gleam coming into his eyes.

"Do you? Do you value pedigree? I have an immensely long pedigree. I can trace my family straight back to Adam—can't you? Or perhaps you can trace yours back to the monkeys? Poor monkeys!" she went on, talikng him down as he essayed so speak. "Oh! it is hard on them! That we should have moved on, and left them still cracking nuts with their teeth and swinging by their tails' Who knows? perhaps they have yearnings that they can't express for patent American nut-crackers, travelling by steam, playing on the concertina, shooting pigeons, dyeing their hair golden, wearing false teeth, and going down in a diving-bell."

"Susie, stop!" cried Mrs. Downay, turning suddenly away from Sir Alfred. "I dislike to hear you running on in that flippant way about a theory that I have a great objection to."

"Very well, my Mèry; suggest something, and I will go on talking about it."

But Mrs. Downay had turned back to Sir Alfred with a slight apology for interrupting him, and she did not answer.

"Would you like to see my dog?" asked Susie in her *youngest* way.

"Oh, certainly, if he does not bite."

Susie rose and left the room, returning in a minute with the lively fox-terrier.

"I call him mine," she said, "but he is not mine; he is my mother's. He was given to her. No one would ever dream of giving a dog to me. But, however, it doesn't matter."

" Why should not some one dream of giving him to you ? You are the very little girl to give a dog to."

" Am I ? Why ?"

" Because I think that you would like a dog much better than a work-box, a book, or, let me see—a fan."

Susie gave a short laugh.

" A work-box, or a book, or a fan ! I did not mean *instead* of anything. Well, never mind. When did you know that you were coming to see us ? Ten minutes before you started ? This morning ? or last night ?"

" I knew it last night. My uncle told me not to let him forget to take or send some grapes to Mrs. Dawnay."

" Oh ! he told you last night," repeated

Susie with an air of satisfaction ; "and you only came in the afternoon, I know, for I saw his phaeton drive past. How long are you going to be here ?"

"I leave the day after to-morrow."

"So soon !" she said, regretfully. "And does Sir Alfred go with you ?"

"I believe so."

"And when are you coming back ?"

"I am not coming back. I shall leave my yacht some time in September, as I go to Scotland."

"Poor yacht ! then it will stop sailing about when you leave it."

"Of course."

Susie asked no more on that score.

"Was your uncle as glad to see you as usual ?" was her next inquiry ; and she actually lifted her eyes to his, with something in their expression odd and pretty, and that pleased him.

"*As usual?*   How glad is he to see me usually when I come ?"

"Oh, very, very, awfully glad !" said Susie, fervently and eagerly.

"Well, I do not think this time he was two 'verys'; he was one."

Susie dropped her eyes, and gave the top of her dog's head a loud kiss. She was smiling.   Eugene began to think her a rather nice little thing.

"You have not asked me the name of my mother's dog," she said.

"But I ask now,—What is his name ?"

"It is spelt S—k—i—p, and pronounced Skip," she answered, with a childish laugh. "I named him ; it is my favourite name for dogs; if I had a dozen they should all be called Skip. What is the name of *your* dog ?"

"I have no dog."

" No dog ! How many friends you must have, then !" she said, in a sad, envious tone.

"You must explain to me what you mean by that."

" People with friends—real friends—can do without the friendship of a dog; but people without friends prize dearly a dog's friendship ; they can hardly live without it." She drew her own dog closer to her as she spoke.

" Surely you have plenty of friends ?"

" None," she replied, looking at him as if she wished her words to sink into his very soul. " Not one."

" Nonsense !"

" Not one," she repeated. " I believe a great many more people would have asked mamma to marry them if it had not been for me."

"Really!" he said, rather taken aback.

"But I think the more they knew of me, you know, the less they would have disliked me. Yes, I could assure any one who married mamma that I would prove no drawback to their happiness." This was said as a most solemn asseveration is made.

"Dear me," said Eugene half to himself, "how very funny."

A misgiving seized Susie that this was not the way to talk of her mother, and that her mother would be shocked and indignant to hear her. Off she went abruptly to another subject. "The birds ate all my strawberries," she remarked, as if this was a piece of intelligence sure to interest him.

"Indeed! That is not doing credit to their early education."

Susie flushed a more vivid scarlet than he thought her pale skin capable of. "You mean that for me!" she said in a tone of uncontrollable anger. " What a home thrust it was!"

" Pray do not imagine anything so thoroughly false and absurd," said Eugene, half scornfully, half in amusement; " my thoughts were quite confined to the birds, I assure you; exclusively."

Susie looked neither convinced nor soothed.

" If it is not too naïf to say it, I must tell you that I think on the contrary that your early education was surely without one flaw."

Susie now did look mollified.

"Then if you mention me," she said, "you will be sure to say that my mother has been able to make a crab walk *almost* straight."

"I shall be sure to mention you, *of course,* but I shall not say that."

" Oh, please do !"

" Very well. At any rate I shall certainly mention that she, or somebody, has taught you to say *please* as prettily as it can be said."

Susie gave Skip a rapturous hug. " Oh !" she exclaimed, " if you would only give me an opportunity to say it again !"

She felt quite carried out of herself, and spoke with the most delightful girlish abandon.

" But, unfortunately, to give you another opportunity I must refuse you something," he answered smiling. " I am afraid you have had your last chance, Miss Susie."

Susie bent her little head shyly down, but not awkwardly now, and felt disagreeably conscious of her limp percale with the white wafers on it. She was blushing, and a tender smile softened the curling corners of her mouth.

"I am afraid that you think me a young lady," she said looking up.   "Do you?"

"No.   Only at the poetic age when brook and river meet."

"Perhaps I am older than you imagine. If I tell you exactly how old I am will you promise faithfully not to tell any one; above all, your uncle?"

"Yes; I promise most faithfully."

"I shall be seventeen in December."

Eugene   looked   genuinely   amazed. "Nearer river than brook." he said.   "I had thought you about fifteen."

"If you had known that I was seventeen, would you have talked to me in the same way?   Said just the same things?"

"Precisely.   Or, no; I do wrong to say that.   I should probably have taken more pains to make an agreeable impression."

"No one has ever gone the right way to

work to make an agreeable impression on
me."

" And what is the right way ? if I may
ask."

" Something the way you have done.
My mother is asking you if you will have a
cup of tea."

When they each had taken their cup,
Susie thought how nice it would be if Mr.
Everard and herself could but take theirs
out under the old apple-tree in the garden
—the only one, which spread out its vener-
able arms as though saying " bless you my
children" to the gooseberry-bushes beside
it. She was judicious enough to refrain
from making any suggestion of the sort,
however, and listened with a stolidity that
she meant should pass for attention, to
a dilapidated old story that Sir Alfred was
telling. Sir Alfred was making himself

agreeable according to his light, which on this point was indeed but a tiny spark.

There was no harm, though, in mentioning that they *had* a garden. At an instant when Sir Alfred's cup was lifted to his lips, she said to Eugene, in an underhand yet emphatic way, "We grow all our own vegetables in our garden."

"How much I should enjoy a dinner or a luncheon with you," he replied, discovering one beauty in her face—thick black curling eyelashes, that gave to her eyes almost a painted look. "Vegetables that you have grown yourself, and things that you have cooked yourself out of a book."

"Oh, come to-morrow," said Susie breathlessly cutting him short. "I promise not to give you cold veal. Once I asked some one to lunch on my own responsibility— asked him to stay on as luncheon time came ; he had ventured to come in the morning ; love makes men very unconventional I think ; mamma was out ; he was hungering for a sight of her ; I was sure that she would be home for luncheon, and since he was reduced to a mere jelly-fish by love, it seemed to me, I thought he would not mind having only cold veal. 'Twas all we had. Mamma staid for lunch somewhere ; she did not come home ; and this unfortunate fellow had only *me* and cold veal. He did try so hard to eat it ; but love and disgust were too much for him. At last he said, as if a shiver were going all down his back, 'Eating cold veal is like kissing one's sister !' "

"And what did you say to that ?"

"Oh, I ?" answered Susie, making demureness a mask from behind which mischief peeped out. " I said, 'There are some

men who, to look at them, I should think,
had never got anything, and could *never*
get anything—but cold veal, so they had
better make the best of it.' Do come to-
morrow ; mamma will be delighted."

"Thanks, I cannot come to-morrow,"
answered Eugene, who had a belief that
his uncle intended asking the widow and
her daughter to lunch at St. Quentin's.

Susie looked excessively disappointed.
"Your manner is so misleading that I actually thought you wanted to come," she
said.

"So I do. My manner is a correct ren-
dering of my feelings. There is a great
charm about this cottage ; I should be delighted to break bread under its roof."

"If you are going the day after to-
morrow you cannot have the delight unless
you come to-morrow."

In her mind Susie had catalogued various
nice things that could appear at their simple board.

"I am not able to come to-morrow."

Susie sighed regretfully. She had
known how frangible were men's engage-
ments when their inclinations and their
acceptances clashed.

"I am sorry," she said, and not in the
icy tone that betokens anger more than
sorrow.

"So am I—rather," he replied with a
smile.

Here was an opportunity for a snub!
But to snub properly there must be an
accumulation of force from preceding irritation, and, except for the last minute,
Susie had never felt so bland in her life.
She had nothing to snub with. There was
no malice in her heart. She was conscious

that her mother had one ear open to her, but no words seethed in her heart and bubbled over at the lips; her heart was like a pool with sunbeams slanting down on it. She was silent, despising herself for hoping that he would say something to take away the flavour of that slighting " rather."

" How do vegetables look when they are growing ?" he inquired, thinking that a stroll round a quaint old garden with this pert child would be rather amusing.

" Potatoes look all top, beans look all pole, asparagus at this season looks all sprangling with red berries; it is growing like Jack's beanstalk, that is the reason. Would you like to come and see it ? I will take out a needle and thread, and string you a handsome coral necklace, if you choose."

"Yes; I choose, decidedly."

He had no sooner spoken than Susie was off, and leaping up the stairs like a kangaroo. She came back with a broad-brimmed garden hat on, trimmed with smart tartan ribbon, and in her hand she carried a bewitching basket full of reels and silks and scissors. On her finger a thimble was already placed. They went away together, round to the back of the house, down a red path fringed by laburnums, and laurels, and laurestinus, into the garden, where a lad was at work on a cucumber frame.

"Young Thomas," Susie said, explanatorily. "Old Thomas, his father, does the heavy gardening, and young Thomas the light. Young Thomas and I work capitally together; he is the very thing for an amateur with fancies, which is what I consider myself. Old Thomas is rooted to his own ideas, but with Young Thomas it is like rolling a ball down a roof. He takes an idea, and off he goes—well, rather too fast."

"Given to works of supererogation, is he ?"

" If you suggest something being pruned, you go out and find that the bush is gone, and that the prunes, or prunings, lying on the ground, are all that is left of it but the roots and a little bit above them. This is the asparagus bed ; I suppose it looks a mere scrap of a thing after your uncle's ?"

"I have never seen my uncle's. I am sure this is large enough to supply two ladies."

" It little dreamed that it was going to supply a gentleman with a necklace," said Susie, seating herself quietly on the neigh-

bouring potato tops, and tearing off a
quantity of red berries. Then she threaded
a large needle, and began stringing the
berries rapidly, Eugene watching her, and
convincing himself that he could not follow
her example, and seat himself on those
waving green tufts.

The light was so deeply rose-coloured,
that it seemed as if it must paint perma-
nently pink the white cheek steeped in
it, and change to ruby the pale coral
lips.

All in green and scarlet as she was, with
her environment of green, and the red
berries in her hand, her little white face
looked as a solitary anemone might in a
large posy of scarlet geraniums and their
leaves.

She quickly strung a long string, and
tied the two ends together.

" Bend down your head," she said, looking up at him.

He did so, and she flung the vegetable ornament over it.

" I dare say you *will* feel a little foolish with it," she said, reading his thoughts, " but please don't take it off. Mary never sees anything that people do in a ludicrous light, unless they mean it to be seen so; she has such a tender heart, and your uncle is not one of the very observing sort; do you think he is ?"

" No; and particularly at present he is not. I will treat this "—touching it—" as I would a V.C., if I had had the bravery to obtain one; that is, I will lay it carefully away, and refresh my spirit by looking at it from time to time; I will treasure it for ever."

Susie watched him as he talked, watched

his smiling lips and his untroubled eyes.

"This is your way of talking to foolish, bird-witted girls," she said, sadly. "I understand exactly what sort of man you are! You '*steal* the sweet forget-me-nots that grow for happy lovers,' and present them, very withered and stale, to people whom you don't care a bit about."

"You are so wise and poetical, that I do not understand you," rejoined Eugene, with arrested attention ; "but I will try and unravel your meaning as we drive home."

He made a step towards the house ; then remembering, turned back again and offered his hand to Susie to help her up. She took it, and rose to her feet.

In after days she recalled the scene, and it would rise before her with the accuracy, the vividness of a photograph.

The old garden, the gaudy light, the string of red berries hanging round Eugene's neck, looking incongruous, and as if he had been playing with a child; the figure of young Thomas tinkering the cucumber frame; her limp percale; Skip enjoying a hidden scent under a gooseberry bush.

They went back to the house, and found Sir Alfred about to take leave.

" Good-bye," said Susie, shaking hands with Eugene. " As you go the day after to-morrow, I suppose I shall not see you again."

He only said good-bye with what Susie in her heart pronounced to be an unfeeling smile.

She did not run to the window to watch the dog-cart drive off, as was her common way : she stood still where she was, with a far-a-way look in her eyes. Looking out with child's eyes on to a woman's future.

"Did you really snub him, Susie?" said her mother softly, and with a little laugh.

"No," answered Susie, dragging down her eye-brows, thrusting out her under lip, sticking her thumbs in her belt and staring down at her shoes.

"My child! don't look so cross. Forget that I asked you; listen to your bird, how sweetly he is singing."

"I don't hear any bird," said Susie without looking up, "I hear a slate pencil scratching on a slate—that is all."

"Poor little dicky!" sighed Mrs. Dawnay, glancing up at the canary piping shrilly in his gilded cage. "Sir Alfred has asked us to lunch with him to-morrow, Susie."

"Has he!" said Susie, with a marvellous change and brightening of expression.

"Oh! I must run out and tell Ann to wash and iron my embroidered white dress; it is the prettiest one I have. Fancy my having this thing on: that looks as if it had come out of a rag-bag!"

"I do not think it matters at all," said the widow laughing.

CHAPTER III.

ALL ON A SUMMER'S DAY.

"IT is not '*steal* the sweet forget-me-nots,' it is 'move the sweet forget-me-nots that grow for happy lovers;' I made a mistake," said Susie. She was standing with Eugene on the terrace of St. Quentin's, waiting with an irritated patience for a peacock to unfold his obstinate tail. "If any one else had misquoted anything so familiar, how I should have laughed at them."

Eugene looked bewildered. "I have not heard you say anything about forget-me-nots," he said.

"Oh, not to-day, yesterday—but you have forgotten."

"Not at all," said Eugene, who obviously had forgotten.

"But you have," insisted Susie in vexation.

"If it was, as you say, some misquotation, then it is just as well that I have," he replied indifferently.

Susie pouted and did not speak for a moment. Then she said, watching the lazy smoke floating reluctantly away from his lips, "I thought it made men good-natured to smoke."

"I think it does; but the companionship of *some people* is even more effectual than smoking the best of cigars," he said, taking his own cigar out of his mouth, and looking into her eyes with a look learned long ago, but dangerously new to her.

" I should like to be over there," she said, after an instant's pause, and pointing as she spoke to verdure and shade and still foliage, where fancy could picture a grey road winding under the embracing tree-boughs, past sleepy mills and broad roofed cottages.

" I will order the phaeton and drive you over if you wish."

" Oh, mamma would never let me go !"

" Nonsense ! we are in Acadia down here. The Acadians never thought any-thing of going off hand in hand anywhere, with their—friends. Or we might have the waggonette and all go. I will ask them."

Mrs. Dawnay was sitting a little distance off with the host and the Rector and his wife, who had also been lunching there.

Eugene said not one word about the waggonette, but he did suggest taking Susie for a drive over to a farm where he had some matter or other to see about. He suggested it as he would have suggested allowing a little boy of four to ride his stick.

Mrs. Dawnay hesitated a moment, and then, disliking to put Susie on a young lady's footing, said, " Yes, she may go ; but please don't let her get out and climb and scramble, Mr. Everard. She does tear her dresses so terribly ; and don't let her be troublesome about stopping to gather this flower, and that flower."

So Susie was driven off in the phaeton, her mother repeating the same injunctions to her that she had given to Eugene. She was driven off with many cautions not to be a troublesome child, and a tomboyish little girl. No one cautioned her not to be a troubled maiden, a womanly young woman.

They scarcely met a living creature : their own voices, their own wheels, the beat of their own horses' hoofs were almost the only sounds that broke the monotony of repose.

Once or twice a dog barked, a bird twittered, a cow lowed; but for that, the pastoral world about them seemed all their own.

Susie, in a white gown, with pale pink roses in her pretty leghorn hat, and paler pink gloves on her little hands, and pink and white striped silk stockings that her coquettish high heeled shoes displayed, looked as Eugene could not have believed her capable of looking. Her heavy hair hung to her waist in curling, dark masses, and in her face was the innocent, rare hap-

piness that does not know itself to be
happiness ; that has not yet been questioned and forced to own, " Yes, I am
happiness—farewell, I fly !"

Through all Susie's words, looks, and
tones ran the prophecy of something to
come infinitely deeper and sweeter than
anything that her life had yet known. Of
her own fore-casting the poor little pro-
phetess herself was unconscious, but the
young man beside her knew, and the knowledge gave her an interest to him that
her unimpressive face could not else have
given.

"That," said she—indicating with her
shell-pink parasol a farm on " uplands airy"
a little bit off—" that is where our butter
and eggs, and some of our fruit come from.
Isn't it a cool, warm, pleasant looking
place ? It looks, I mean, as if it must be

cool in summer, warm in winter, and pleasant always."

" Let us see it a little nearer," said Eugene turning the horses abruptly off into a
rough looking road apparently leading up
to it.   "Should you like to live on a farm?"

" Oh, no ; milk and cream make mamma
bilious.   Why, you are driving up to it !"

" Yes ; I want to speak to Jarrett about
something ; and perhaps they will give us
a glass of milk.. Milk and cream do not
make *me* bilious."

" Nor me."

They drove up to the old grey front
of the house where passion-flowers, pale
and starry, were clinging and trembling.

At the sound of the wheels a little Blenheim spaniel came out barking furiously.
This brought a girl of eleven, with shaggy
hair and enormous elastic-side boots, with

two great straps prominently sticking out at the ankle of each. She stared wonderstruck at the pink and white lady, the handsome young gentleman, and the immovable groom, who, as the horses came to a standstill was immovable no longer, but out and at their heads.

" Where is your father ?" said Eugene to this damsel. "I should like to see him."

" Feyther's in the house," answered the girl pointing over her shoulder.

Eugene jumped out. " You will not mind waiting here for half a second," he said to Susie, and disappeared within the porch. Though why one whom Susie considered so fine a gentleman should have gone to the farmer, and not desired the farmer to come to him, she really could not determine.

He was gone thousands of half seconds ;

and when he came out it was with a mug of milk in his own hand. The farmer stood behind him; his rustic comeliness seeming a poor and homely thing enough, when compared with the beauty of young Dives in front of him.

Eugene held the milk up to her, and she drank half; it was a large ale mug; he drank the rest; and this token of non-fastidiousness where she was concerned caused Susie a delightful blush. She even noticed that where her lips had pressed his did too, and wondered if that was accident or intention. He handed the mug to the farmer, and getting in beside Susie, nodded a good-day to him. "You understand, then?" he said as he drove off.

"Oh yes, sir, I understand."

Susie would have liked to let loose a whole pack of questions on him; for the most insignificant thing he could do was fraught with interest to her. But she forbore, that she might not be obliged to torture herself with self-upbraiding and dissatisfaction to-night when her head should be on the pillow. She wished that there should be nothing to afterwards make herself uncomfortable about in the whole of this completely satisfying day.

For her to feel as if she had achieved a great triumph, a great success,—feel as if she was a beautiful young conqueror instead of an unpretending over-flattered girl, was perhaps more due—far more due—to his being a past master in the art of pleasing, than to her artlessness in being over pleased by a handsome young man of the world who had been at some little pains to make himself remembered by her.

It was so late that he drove her to her

own home, and not to St. Quentin's ; he got out himself, saying that he would come in and bid adieu to Mrs. Dawnay as he had not already done so. They entered the house by the drawing-room window.

" Mamma is not in the house ; I *feel* that she is not," said Susie the instant her foot crossed the threshold. " I daresay she has gone back with Mrs. Hay for afternoon tea."

" I am sorry," replied Eugene—" sorry not to say good-bye to your charming mother. We leave to-morrow morning early. Will you say good-bye to her for me ?"

" Yes," said Susie.

" Good-bye," holding out his hand to her and smiling.

Susie took the hand, making a little curtsying movement as she did so ; a half genuflection it was.

Certainly, thought Eugene, if her face was faulty her grace was faultless.

"Keep a small corner in your memory for me," he said, with a gaiety that robbed his words of all sweetness for Susie.

"Well, I will; a very little bit of a scrap of a corner," she replied in exactly his own tone; "and you keep the order I bestowed on you; if I ever see you again I shall ask, you if you have it."

Eugene looked amused; the trashy thing was not even now in his possession; what had become of it he knew not.

"You haven't it now!" cried Susie, with speedy intuition, and frowning at him.

"Ask me if I have not ten years from now, and see what I will answer," he said, impressively, and relinquishing her hand as he spoke. "Good-bye, again."

"Good-bye," said Susie, coolly, and turning away.

He crossed the little lawn, and she heard the sound of his wheels as he drove off and was gone.

She was pouting, frowning, reddening. "Asparagus berries!" said she. "How disgusting the two words sound. Why not have given him a turnip, or a nice melon scooped out, with eyes, nose, and mouth cut in it, to remember me by?"

She threw off her hat, tore off her gloves, and seating herself at the piano, began to play " Tam O'Shanter" with unnecessary clatter, as if she herself were pursued by witches whose name was Legion.

CHAPTER IV.

"WHIPS AND STINGS."

"AND about those bills, Susie? Have you added them together?"

This was one day in September, and poor Mrs. Dawnay made the query in a very timorous tone.

"Oh! don't mention them," said Susie, throwing them down on the floor, leaning her head back, and closing her eyes as she would have done if any one had been beating a dog or hurting a bird in her pre-

sence. " That box of dresses from Paris,"
she said, after a miserable pause, opening
her eyes with an effort, and speaking tra-
gically, " I wish they were all at the bottom
of the sea !"

" I wish they were back in Paris again ;
I do, indeed," sighed the widow. " Imagine
her daring to put real lace on the petti-
coats !"

" And our having to pay for it," added
Susie. " I should not have minded her
daring to put it on, if only we had not to
pay for it. Then the butcher, the baker,
the candlestick-maker ! Why, I thought
you could live for nothing, or next to nothing, down in the country—the real,
honest country ; and we with our own
vegetables and our own cow ! It really
is horrible to think of what we owe
in one way and another ; living in such

a simple little way as we have done,
too."

"And how much *do* we owe, Susie?"
asked her mother, trembling.

"Seven hundred pounds, eleven shillings,
and sixpence," said Susie, with slow intensity.

"Oh, Susie!"

"And oh, Mèry! the cow, you know, the
jardinières, and piano, and gilded chairs,
and things; the copper casseroles, and ket-
tles and pans, and rolling-pins and skillets,
and spice-boxes, and all the tricks of the
trade; the glass all over fern-leaves; the
new tea-cups and things that they sent for
from Newport for us; the new carpets and
curtains. Why, I don't believe you realize
that we have all but refurnished the house.
Then our mere eating and drinking are as
expensive, it seems to me, as if we were a

family of ten. Yes, ten grown-up men;
all *bons-vivants.*"

" No, no," said Mrs. Dawnay, depre-
catingly. " And what are we to do ?"

There was no answer from Susie, except
in a tone that would have been a fit con-
comitant for wailing and gnashing of teeth.
" Those dresses !"

There came another pause, then it was
Susie who said, " What are we to do ?"

" Yes ; what *are* we to do ?" said the
widow, with mournful reiteration.

" We must do something," said Susie,
unsuggestively.

" Yes ; but what ?"

Still another pause.

" It doesn't sound very much," said
Susie ; " seven hundred pounds eleven
shillings and sixpence. Don't I make it
sound small, mother ?"

"No, no; not when I know what our account is at our bankers."

"And how are we to manage?"

"How, indeed, when our whole income for a year will not pay it?"

"I can feel it making wrinkles on my forehead," said Susie, rubbing her hand up and down on her baby brow.

"It is a very dreadful thing to be deeply in debt without any idea of how and when you can get out again," said Mrs. Dawnay, in a troubled voice. "And I believe that after giving a year's credit they charge five per cent. interest."

"I feel as if I were at sea in a bowl!" cried Susie, starting up and beginning to walk distractedly up and down the room, her glance bent moodily on her smart shoes and silk stockings fresh from Paris.

"There is but one thing to be done that

I can see," said Mrs. Dawnay, with a sad deliberateness. "We must write to your Aunt Adria."

Aunt Adria was a sister of Mr. Dawnay, who had married a Mr. Willis many years ago. A rich man, but beneath her in birth. So much beneath her, according to the family idea, that the only way to receive him was to make a feud over him. Mr. Dawnay had been conservative, and for his conservatism his sister had been grateful, and Mrs. Dawnay knew it.

Susie drew back her head with a gesture of intense pride, and stopped short in her promenade amongst the furniture.

"Horrible!" she said, dismembering the word, and lingering over each little syllable. "I—intend—I intend to ask Sir Alfred to help us."

"Susie! you will never do that."

"Yes, I shall—to-day if he comes; and I suppose he will—he hardly ever skips a day now."

Susie rushed out of the room before she had quite finished speaking. In all her life she had never disobeyed her gentle mother; and if her mother had now forbidden her she must have yielded; she could not disobey her; she would have believed that some dreadful evil would overtake her should she do so.

She rushed out of the room, and out of the house, and out of the garden-gate too; scampering down the road, and down a lane, and into a well-known favourite copse, as fast as her feet could carry her. She did not go back for luncheon; indeed, she felt as if it would be meritorious on her part never to eat again, but to live on air like an orchid, for air certainly costs nothing. She

stole home about three o'clock, and, entering the drawing-room, looked about her
with a woe-begone face, fearing to find her
lovely but indebted mother either in tears
over her liabilities, or sitting with a satin
cheek on a satin hand, and a book upside
down on her lap, brooding, with melancholy
eyes fixed on vacancy.

The room was cool, perfumed, and still,
except for a softly recurring sound coming
from a luxurious sofa in the darkest
corner. There lay Mrs. Dawnay, calmly
asleep, her golden head lying easily on the
down, lace-covered cushion, a magazine sitting on its half-open leaves on the floor
beside her where it had tumbled, rose-leaves
from an over-ripe rose in her belt drifting
over her.

With great relief and satisfaction Susie
took a book she was reading softly from the

table, and went tip-toeing out to the seat
in the laurel's shade, where she established
herself, and soon became enthralled in
" Eva."

The click of the garden gate made her
look up; there was Sir Alfred advancing
over the grass towards her.

" Ah !" he said, coming beside her, " stu-
dious Miss Susie; ' Eva,' and in the origi-
nal—unruly member ! accomplished Miss
Susie !"

Susie looked up into his withered old
face, and the violent throbs of her heart
seemed to be saying to her, "Seven hundred
pounds eleven shillings and sixpence."
Could she ask him for help ?

" Sir Alfred," she faltered out, and
paused. No—impossible ! It was easier
to appeal to kith and kin, after all, than to
a stranger like this. " Mamma is asleep, or

was asleep, Sir Alfred," she said, in her usual tone; "Let me run in and see if she is awake."

But the widow, who had heard her guest's voice, came out herself, flushed from sleep, smiling, and looking lovely in her beautiful new dress.

"What a fool I should have been to ask him," thought Susie, quite gloating over the baronet's enraptured gaze. "As if it was not all coming out perfectly right for us. I sha'n't let her write to Aunt Adria—hateful old cast-iron image! Indeed my Mèry shall not write. I must finish this alone," she said, honestly enough, "for I am going to cry over it. I peeped at the end, and it is so, *so* sad! I am going to cry dreadfully over it, and I do not like for any one to see me cry."

She went away with her book; and

among the seedy vegetables, the currant and
gooseberry bushes of the ugly old garden,
let loose the flood of her sympathy and
sorrow over her unfortunate heroine, to
whom fate and man were implacable.

" Whose griefs have you really been crying over, sweet one ?" asked Mrs. Dawnay,
as they seated themselves at the dinner-
table—" your own, or Eva's ?"

" Oh, her's—poor Eva's !" said Susie ;
" ours will come out all right, I dare say.
Do not write to Aunt Adria, mamma ; at
least, not quite yet."

" I have already written."

" You have not sent the letter ?"

" But I have.   I wrote while you were
out—you were gone a very long time, Susie
—and young Thomas has taken the letter
to post."

Susie pushed back her chair from the
table, grief and indignation in her face.

" Wrote without letting me see the letter ? Oh, mother !"

" I have kept a copy of it for you to see, dear. I have done quite right ; it was the only thing to do. I do not very much mind being in debt to Adria ; but these people ! —I cannot *live* and feel that I am dealing unjustly by people whose trade gives them their daily bread. I blame myself more than words can say for going on so reck- lessly. Why did I not think ? But I do so love pretty things !" This was the conclu- sion, with a sigh.

" And so do I," said Susie, going on with her dinner, "I dote on them ; and I thought one could live in the heart of the country for just nothing at all. Well ! there is a bubble burst !" The end of this sentence, too, was a sigh.

A few mornings after this conversation

took place, a letter came from Scotland to Mrs. Dawnay. She opened it, and out of it dropped a cheque ; after glancing at it she handed it to Susie ; and Susie saw that they were almost righted.

" Now for the letter," she said ; " let us hear what Aunt Adria has to scold."

Mrs. Dawnay began to read ; and after going as fast as she could through the severities and cold amenities of the first part, read very much slower and more carefully as she drew near the end of the letter.

" Susie's education must have been very imperfectly attended to," wrote the lady, " with your unsettled life, small means, and extravagant tastes, and I suppose that advantages for her in the place where you now are, there are absolutely none. Mr. Willis and I have a proposition to make to you, and it is that you shall allow her to come to us in London, in November, for nine months or a year, to share with our Alice the masters, etc., with whom she is finishing her education, before being presented in the spring. Susie shall be very welcome, and you will thus be spared all expense as regards her, for, of course, in dress and all other little matters she will be our charge. A horse will be provided for her, that she may accompany Alice in her rides. Health, conduct, and deportment all shall be attended to," and so, with a few more curt sentences, the letter came to an end.

The mother and daughter looked at one another without speaking for a full minute. Susie then took up the cheque and fingered it.

" Very kind of her to send us this," she said.

" Very," echoed the widow, in a heart-sick voice.

" Had I better go, mother, do you think ? Oh, mother, say no !"

" My heart says no, daughter dear ; but my common sense says yes.   It is the very thing that I should like above all others to do ; to go up to town and have the best of finishing masters and mistresses for you ; to have you ride every day on a well-appointed horse ; to have you made, in fact, into one of the most graceful and ac-complished of girls.   That is impossible.   I cannot go with you ; I can afford none of it.   The want of money is the root of much evil.   Nine months or a year would soon pass.   Perhaps I might manage to come up and go into lodgings in March or April, and so see you again."

" No, I will not go, mamma !"—with a

desperate effort to speak quietly, and a deep blush—"do not be angry with me, or shocked at me, but I have a sort of fancy that we may some day go to St. Quentin's to live, so why need we separate? Anybody must be blind not to see how—how—in fact, I think that any day now Sir Alfred may ask you to come and live for ever at St. Quentin's."

"You will of course give up this idea when I tell you what I had not intended to tell you, but which you force me into doing. Sir Alfred has already asked me. He asked me the last time he was here."

"And you refused?"

Her mother looked at her steadily, and slightly bowed her head.

Susie bent down her's, saying to herself, as the blood leaped into brow and cheeks "Another bubble burst!"

Presently she looked up, and speaking with perfect calmness, said,

" I am wretched at the thought of leaving you, mamma, but if you would promise to come up in March or April, I think I can manage to make myself willing to go."

" That is right, Susie; yes, it is quite right; but what shall I do without you?"

Susie ran to her, clasping her round the neck, and raining kisses on her soft cheek.

" All alone down here! Oh, I cannot go away and leave you!"

" What, not from November till March? Yes you can, dear, and you must. I shall be separated from you just long enough not to actually sicken for a sight of you, and then I shall see you again. It is very good and thoughtful of Adria."

" Why couldn't she have asked you to come ? I should think she would have remembered how you would be left down here in the dull, dead country, all alone."

Mrs. Dawnay shook her head with a smile.

" That would have been quite too much," she said. " It is very kindly thought of, and kindly done of Adria. It will be very nice for you, Susie."

CHAPTER V.

KITH AND KIN.

ON a calm, sunny, November day, the mother and daughter stood on Ryde pier bidding one another farewell. They did it with commendable self-control; yet Susie felt wretched enough, and so, too, did her mother. They could hardly bear to finally unlock their clinging, trembling hands, and separate; but it was done at last. Susie stumbled down the sanded steps behind the rector's wife, who had taken charge of her to town, and went on board the boat. Mrs. Dawnay leaned over the pier railing to see the last of her one chicken.

There she was, a girlish, graceful figure, with eager, unconscious gestures of farewell. There was but one person in the world to her at that minute, and that one was her mother.

" How lonely your mamma will be without you," said Mrs. Hay, half way over, wrapping herself warmly in a shawl.

" Oh, Mrs. Hay," cried Susie, bending towards her eagerly, " don't let her be very lonely; go and see her very, *very* often, won't you ?"

" Certainly I will; it is always a pleasure. I promise you that I will quite overrun her, and I intend to make great calls on her time and charity for my poor people, too ; she shall almost forget to miss you, my dear."

At the Victoria Station, Susie parted from Mrs. Hay, and entered a brougham that had come to meet her, and while the good lady went bumping off in a four-wheeler, with all her goods and chattels a-top, her young charge was rolled springingly away in blissful carelessness as to her effects. Extreme thoughtlessness made Susie eminently fitted to be a fine lady.

She had only had peeps at London while passing through it, and looked out of the window with a good deal of interest as she went rapidly along. It was a still, mild day, and a number of people were abroad. Down through the wide streets of Belgravia and Kensington-wards they went, to pause at last before a great, new-looking house, fronting the east.

Susie got out, entered the open door, and went up-stairs. She was shown into a small bright room with one occupant. The one occupant was a fair-haired blooming girl, with eyebrows as arched as crescent moons. She had on a coquettish muslin apron, with pockets and blue bows, and on the apron lay a little Blenheim spaniel, which she was combing with a broken ivory comb.

As Susie entered, she pushed the dog off, threw down the comb, and, rising, met her cousin half-way with some speech of welcome, followed by an embrace and kiss. The cousins had not seen each other since they were young children.

" I will show you your room," said Alice Willis. " Mamma will be sorry not to have been here when you arrived. She will be back now at any moment."

As she spoke she went out of the room and upstairs, Susie following her. Her room was pretty and comfortable-looking; but the aching in her heart that the separation from her mother caused, made nothing seem enjoyable or even satisfactory to her.

She began mechanically taking off her hat and jacket, her cousin watching her, and noting that the warm, close-fitting travelling dress had the *cachet* of a French dressmaker. She picked up one of Susie's gloves that had fallen to the floor. "What sized gloves do you wear?" she asked.

"Sixes," said Susie.

"Why, I take six and a quarter!"

"Do you?" said Susie, indifferently.

"And I daresay you can wear boots as small as mine; I wear threes."

"Oh, I wear twos."

"Really!" (Miss Willis considered the word 'really' to be all that any occasion demanded, from news of the downfall of a dynasty to the price of a new bonnet.) "But then size of feet and hands is all a matter of proportion; I am five feet five," drawing herself up.

"So am I," said Susie, beginning to bathe her face in the chilly water.

"So! you can wash your face?"

"Of course I can: you don't imagine that I would let anyone wash it for me?"

"Some girls cannot, unless they can have a thorough re-making up afterwards. Marble white girls come out shining red girls I can assure you."

"Dreadful!" exclaimed Susie, forgetting her mother for an instant. "I am not made up; but you can tell that at a glance, without my taking the trouble to inform

7—2

you.—Oh, who are these? Cora and Lucy?" for two little girls, one eleven, and one eight, had come into the room.

" Yes, Cora and Lucy."

Susie kissed them, and asked them if they knew who she was.

" Oh yes," they both answered; she was Susie—Cousin Susie, who had come to live with them.

The younger one, Lucy, was holding the little King Charles in her arms.

" Is he yours?" asked Susie.

"Oh no," came in a chorus from the three. " He is mine," " He is Alice's."

" Where did you get him?" said Susie.

The little ones looked at Alice.

Alice let her white eyelids fall, with a half smile and conscious blush.

" He was given to me—sent to me," she murmured; " I love him to distraction!"

She snatched the dog from her sister, and began kissing his little head violently.

" The giver ought to hear you," returned Susie, with not too much toleration. " Ought to hear what you say, and ought to hear those kisses. He or she could, if they were in the street, and the window open. I never heard kisses that sounded so like the cracking of a whip."

Alice raised her head, and regarded her cousin with speechless surprise and indignation.

Susie was not aware of having said anything offensive. Little Cora giggled, showing two rows of small pearly teeth. Lucy, watching her opportunity, darted forward and seized the spaniel, who yelped at the roughness of her grasp.

" Take him out," said Alice, shortly ; " I hate to hear him yelp."

" Susie !" said a voice at the door, " you have come !"

A lady entered, tall, stiff, and slight, with worn features, and strange eyes, like an angry parrot's.

" Yes, Aunt Adria, here I am," and Susie met Mrs. Willis half way, holding up pursed lips, like a child, to be kissed, her full round tones contrasting with the melancholy cadences of her aunt, who spoke like one in a miserable dream.

The questions she asked her niece, the various speeches she made to her, were with far-away glances, and uttered with the monotonous evenness of a woman drugged to apathy.

But she meant to be kind ; and with welcoming words dying faintly on her lips, left the room as noiselessly as she had entered it.

A maid came to unpack Susie's boxes. Alice seated herself comfortably and looked on, talking meanwhile of vanities. Susie had thought herself rather given over to the love of millinery, but she discovered that as a cup full of water is to the ocean, was her love of finery when compared with her cousin's.

At the sound of the dressing-bell Alice rose.

" We are to dine to-night. I thank the spirits there is not a séance. What is the use of dressing and looking well only to sit in the dark ?"

" A séance ? Is Aunt Adria a spirit-ualist ?"

" We dabble in it. But do not be afraid ; you will not be bored by it. Mamma is most anxious to know what happens to us after the sad event——"

" By the ' sad event,' I suppose you mean dying ?" interrupted Susie.

" Yes. She is miserable in thinking of the separation of friends. It is a sad thought, you see, to feel that they go no-where, and that we are parted from them——"

" Yes," cried Susie, " but there is one sadder still : I don't want to part from *Susie,*" hugging herself affectionately.

Alice at that moment was furtively look-ing at herself in the glass.

" When some women look in the glass," said Susie, " it is to be hoped that they go away and straightway forget what manner of women they are."

" Do you mean because they are so ugly ?" asked Alice, crimsoning.

" Yes."

" Did you intend that for *me,* then ?"

continued Alice, her voice trembling with anger.

"No, no! I never thought of such a thing. Oh, my speeches are unlucky!"

"You *are* malapropos," said Alice, in tart assent, and left the room.

"Oh, Alice!" cried Susie, pursuing her out into the passage, "Of course I did not mean you; you are *anything* but ugly; you are as pretty as——"

"Hallo, hallo!" said a firm masculine voice in the half-darkness, "who is this, shouting compliments to Alice at the top of their lungs?"

"It is I," said Susie, sneakily, "Susie."

"Oh!" said the voice, nearer now; "come and let me look at you. I am your Uncle Willis. We have yet to make each other's acquaintance."

He moved under the gas as he spoke,

and Susie following him, they shook hands, and saw each other's faces.

Mr. Willis looked as if he had been adding up figures all his life. His manner was cheerful, almost jocular; it was only when he said "Ha-ha!" and made it do duty for a laugh, that one knew he would like to take a long holiday from life.

"I was only speaking to Alice," said Susie, explanatorily.

"Where is she? I do not see her," said Mr. Willis, looking about him.

"I don't know," returned Susie, blankly. "I suppose she has gone to her room."

Mr. Willis stared, said "Ha, ha!" and passed on.

As his footsteps died away, an opposite door was cautiously opened, and Alice's blonde head thrust out. "This is my room," said she; "come and see it."

" But, after all," said Susie, stepping in, " it does not much matter whether one is pretty or not, since by the time one is fifty, time has stripped us of our good looks."

" Oh, you are still on the same theme," rejoined Alice, after looking at her for an instant in perplexity. " I have often thought," she continued, pensively, " if I were given my choice of growing ugly *fatly*, or growing ugly *thinly*, which I should select."

" I should rather be thin," said Susie, unhesitatingly. " Being thin may have a tragic side, but not a comic, as being fat has. There is nothing ridiculous and laughable in attenuation, but there is in huge quantities of flesh ; it makes one *un objet pour rire.*"

" You are right. But on the other hand bones are pathetic. I am not sure that it is not better to make people feel like laughing, rather than crying."

" There would be no indecision in *my* mind, were I to be given a choice," said Susie. " But I must go back and dress. I should think you might have your wish, and grow *enormously* fat. I know a lady who looks now like a white whale ; when she was young I can imagine that she looked like you."

So Susie, in all simplicity and speaking, took her departure from the room.

CHAPTER VI.

WHILST THOU LIVEST, KEEP A GOOD TONGUE IN THY HEAD.

IT only took twenty-four hours for Susie to permeate the moral atmosphere of her new home.

She was like a small galvanic battery, giving shocks to the self-love, the egoism, of each member of the Willis family.

Her sinewy frankness, her bald truthfulness were as irrepressible as the moon's changes. The only thing to be done, as snubbing failed, was to submit to her.

Mrs. Willis, involved in chimeras of unseen worlds, and an unknown existence, was quite out of sympathy with her niece's youthful realism.

Susie drifted through a dim, moist, November day, side by side with these vessels of various fabrics; managing to jostle even against the little pipkin, Lucy.

There was a morning walk with the two younger girls and their governess, Miss Wix, Alice meanwhile taking a ride.

Kensington Gardens, in depressing Quakerish dress, was selected as usual by Miss Wix, and here Susie scampered about a little with the children, to the admiration of beholders.

One beholder, a tall dark man, striving to accomplish the difficult feat of watching without appearing to look, was seen through by Susie, who desisted from her gambols, and limited herself to a quick walk. An Italian lesson with her cousin occupied a part of the afternoon, and so the gray hours wore away.

Alice and she were to dine late, and in the evening there was to be a séance.

Now, at six o'clock all four cousins were collected in Susie's room. The two little girls, not having as yet much self-love to be wounded—self-love being among those other tormenting acquirements which add to the burthen and weight of accumulating years—were on the road to loving their cousin very dearly, notwithstanding her bluntness.

Alice was bewailing her hard fate of dressing and looking " decent," to sit in the dark nearly all the evening.

" But you will not *dine* in the dark," said Susie, cheeringly. " And if I get an opportunity, I will tell my neighbour in the circle to observe your contour."

" I will thank you to say nothing about me. I am already horribly afraid of your glaring statements. Why, you would be very likely to say that I was vain."

" No, no ; I should never say that you were vain," said Susie, in the earnest, hearty manner which carried conviction with it.

Alice's face took on more than its usual complacent, stall-fed look.

"But," continued Susie, in the same round, sturdy tone, "if any one were to say that you were vain, I should not contradict them."

" If any one were to say to me that you were a sort of human porcupine, I should not contradict them," rejoined Alice calmly, but with quick-winking eyes. When she was annoyed she always winked an incredible number of times in a minute.

" You would be right," said Susie, cheerfully. " Look at Charlie ; he *smells* that you are angry."

" I am not angry."

" Dogs *smell* anger, grief, death, dishonesty, beggary, kindness, treachery. I wonder what the scent of them is like ? Who did you say gave him to you, Alice ?"

" I merely said that he had been made a present to me," answered Alice, with her conscious smile.

" Oh, beg pardon. I didn't know it was a secret."

" It is not a secret."

" Alice does get so red and hot and silly looking whenever she says Mr. Everard's name : no wonder she does not want to say it," observed little Miss Cora, in a tone of the tenderest commiseration.

"Mr. Everard,—Mr. Eugene Everard? do you know him?" asked Susie, turning sharply on Alice.

"Yes; do *you*?" with counter astonishment. "He often joins me when I ride, and he has dined here several times. Where on earth did you meet him? On the Continent?"

"No; his uncle lives near us, and he came to spend a day or two with him."

"Do you know his uncle well?"

"Yes, rather," said Susie, laconically.

"You cannot know Mr. Everard 'yes, rather,' though, if he was only there a day or two. Do you think him handsome?"

"Very."

"And agreeable?"

"He is a humbug, and humbugs are *very* agreeable."

"What do you mean when you say a humbug? A story-teller?"

"No; a pretty speech-maker."

"Oh, how red you are!" put in Cora, pointing straight into her sister's flushed face.

Alice struck down the little hand.

"Rude child!" she said. "I shall tell mamma how rude and unmannerly you are. —Pray, what did he make pretty speeches about to you, Susie? Did he tell you you were as beautiful as a Houri? or as learned as a somebody or other?"

"Of course not. I should not call crude, downright things like that pretty speeches. I don't remember now exactly what he said, but I remember perfectly well the impression he made on me.—Look at him wriggling his dear little snub nose about, he smells the dinner. There is the dressing-bell, Alice."

Alice departed, seizing the dog from the bed by the back of the neck as she went, and carrying him off, kicking convulsively.

The children ran away after their sister. Susie seated herself before the glass; her hands listlessly clasped, her eyes fixed on the carpet. They knew him then. At any time she might see him. And Alice was a blonde beauty.

CHAPTER VII.

A NEW SENSATION.

" Wealthy and proud was he :
He had all that was worth a wish on earth."

RANICAR HUNGERFORD had been everywhere, seen everything, done everything, exhausted all the emotions; and now, at six and thirty, was beset with an ennui so afflicting, that often, if he had happened to be a woman instead of a man, he would have shed tears of weariness and self-pity.

He had been in love several times, but had never yet seen the woman whom he

seriously wished to make his wife. He had
been in many places that, for a little while,
he had thought enchanting; but he never
yet had been in one that he sincerely desired
to make his home. His first thought on
opening his eyes of a morning, was " How
am I ever to get through this day ? with
its hours that no clock measures as I
measure ?"

For time now appeared to him to be an
invention of the Arch-Enemy; from which
there was no escape except into eternity,
and eternity, strange to say, he trembled at,
from the very conviction that once to be on
its dim and boundless shores was never
more to be " bored."

He was good-looking, and would have
been better looking if he had not had a
famished look in his dark, shadow-circled
eyes. He had seen so many men make

fools of themselves with their imitation of the Sir Charles Coldstream manner, their affectation of being bored to death, their constant forcing upon people that they had found their doll stuffed with sawdust,—that it was one of the few aims of his life never to appear devoured by ennui, as he always was in reality.

He was in London in the dreary month of November, en passant, and was trying to decide how to dispose of the long, coming winter. Trying to decide whether he should feel less desperately tired to stay where he was, or to rove from one gay capital to another in search of the diversion which he had long ago ceased to find. English country house life he detested.

One morning he was seated at the breakfast table, idly balancing a sovereign on the tip of his finger, thinking that the best way to

decide about " go " or " stay " was to toss up
—when Eugene Everard entered the room.

Mr. Hungerford smoothed his brow,
smiled, and greeted his guest as civilly as a
man can who has a deep, unspeakable
grudge against another.

" What are you going to do this evening?" asked Eugene in the course of conversation. " I suppose that just now you are
not very busy."

" I am never very busy. I always like
the theatre; I was thinking of going to the
Gaiety, to-night, to have a laugh to sleep
on."

"I think I can give you a new sensation,
perhaps ; I am going to a séance to-night ;
come with me."

" Why do you think that I want a new
sensation ?" asked Ranicar, tenaciously,
"the old ones are quite enough for me, I

assure you. Besides, I do not think I
should like the heat and crowd, and elbow-
ing and vulgar agitation."

"There will be nothing of the sort at this
séance, for it is at the house of some friends
—acquaintances—of mine. Everything will
be done to the scent of flowers and sound
of slow music. You will only come in con-
tact with—the little fingers of the daughter
of the house, perhaps, as your hand touches
hers, and you may come away with some
new ideas concerning your ancestors ; for
instance, that your respected grandfather
has found his affinity in the spirit world to
be Ninon de l'Enclos, or something of that
sort ; but if you have any curiosity to hear
what it is pretended are communications
from the souls of the dead, come by all
means."

" I should much prefer having a commu-

nication from my own ghostly inhabitant;
however, I dare say that it will amuse me
very much, so I will come. Who are the
people, and where do they live?"

Eugene told him; and then the talk
drifted off to other matters.

They went to the Willises together that
evening. Mrs. Willis was only too delighted
to have such a man brought as Ranicar
Hungerford; so well known and much
thought of was he. As for Alice, she was
in a flutter; and, while Ranicar was speaking to her mother, murmured, in smothered
elation, a list of his excellencies to Susie.
Susie caught the words " Show place in
——shire—clever,—wrote—the one with
the grey cover, you know. Hugely rich."
Then he was brought over and introduced,
and she managed cleverly to get him quite
away from Susie, and have him all to
herself.

Eugene stayed by Susie. " Cut out !" thought Susie, looking after Alice and Mr. Hungerford.

" Why did I not see you yesterday afternoon when I called ?" asked Eugene. " I heard then that you were here. I was very much surprised."

" I know you were here," said Susie.

He waited for her to go on, but, finding that she did not mean to do so, said in a tone of suave regret—

" I am sorry that you did not think me worth coming down for."

Susie did not answer ; indeed, she would have found no listener. For Eugene, as well as every one else, had turned to look at the two people who had come to furnish the evening's entertainment.

Mr. Van Vleck and his niece, Miss Médor. But where the others stared in moderation

Eugene was agog ; the man he overlooked ;
it was the girl who chained his attention,
not solely by her beauty, but by his belief
that he and she had met before,—in a moment he had remembered when and where.
It matters not to you, reader.

Having recalled the occasion, he forgot
all else but her lissome grace, and the
Creole beauty that masked her soul.

Mr. Van Vleck (an American, whose
home was on the border of fair Lake
Winnipesauke) introduced his niece with
evident pride.

She crouched a courtesy ; swaying back
amongst her black draperies until her face
looked like—

"A flower worked on black crape."

No motion could have been more supple
and sinuous.

Her hands were noticeable. It was not

a fat, dimpled hand, such as a promoted milkmaid might have—a hand with pulpy knuckles ; it was lean, smooth, sinewy ; like the hand of an American Indian.

All the people who had come sharp-set for the supernatural were eager to commence operations. The footmen, carrying a table, made their appearance through the folding doors ; chairs were arranged, and they took their places.

The girl medium sat between Susie and Mrs. Willis.

There were to be, first of all, written communications, therefore the lamps were left burning.

A sheet of paper was placed under Miss Léontine Médor's hand ; a pencil between her fingers. There was a breathless waiting. Hungerford, who sat on Susie's other side, thought he had never seen two profiles offer a sharper contrast to each other than Miss Médor's and Susie's. Susie's naïf, wide-eyed, lily-pale, with parted, dewy lips; watchful, attent. The other with sleek brown features, every muscle drilled to deceive. The line of the lips stark and motionless, but of a feverish red; the long black lashes sweeping a smooth creamy cheek. Miss Médor was a Creole.

Presently he felt his nervous little neighbour thrill. Strange spirals like corkscrews had begun to make their appearance on the paper.

"Who that has entered the spirit life, related to those present, wore curls?" asked Mr. Van Vleck in a deep voice.

A solemn silence prevailed.

"Grandma Dawnay wore a frisette, with bunches of little curls," said Susie, in a small, trembling voice.

Miss Médor slowly turned towards her.

" A message is coming from her to you," she said in a low, impressive tone.

" Oh dear ! oh dear !" said Susie, extremely perturbed. " Is there ?" Then, suddenly : " I don't believe it. Grandma Dawnay would never take the trouble to send me a message. Why, she said that she would rather have a plague of grass- hoppers than *me* staying in the house with her again !"

Mr. Van Vleck bit his lip savagely. Miss Médor's brown skin paled. People looked inclined to laugh.

" Susie," said Mrs. Willis, in an awful voice, " if you are going to treat a solemn subject with levity, I beg that you will leave the circle."

" This young lady has broken the com- munication," said Mr. Van Vleck. " It will be useless to proceed with this branch of our occult—hum! ha!"

And on this, he got up and lowered all the lamps. Returning, what strange sounds became audible! Crepitations and thumps, celestial music on the concertina, bells tinkling.

"I am frightened!" said Susie, quaveringly.

"I hope you're scared out of a year's growth," muttered Mr. Van Vleck to himself.

"Pray leave the room," said Mrs. Willis, with irritation.

Susie rose to her feet and began to glide away. To her surprise, Hungerford did the same.

"Let me come with you," he said; "I am tired of this——"

On their way through the semi-darkness

they came upon another figure, moving quietly. It was Eugene ; and he seated himself beside Léontine in Susie's stead.

In the adjoining room it was bright and cheerful. There was Mr. Willis reading, with one ear evidently turned on the dark doings next door, after which he had a hankering that he would not confess.

" This is Mr. Hungerford, Uncle Willis," said Susie, " we came out because I was frightened, and he did not believe in it."

" Believe in it ! I should think not," said Mr. Willis ; " as great nonsense as ever came meandering from Tophet."

Susie and Ranicar seated themselves. Ranicar wondered why he did not go home and go to bed, since he was not amused.

Terrible rappings and thumpings and discordant airs on the piano came from the next room. Susie, feeling safe here in the light, smiled. Mr. Willis, unable longer to abstain from joining in the grim fun, jumped up and vanished through the folding doors.

Ranicar yawned and pulled his moustache down, trying to quench it.

Susie turned as pink as the inside of a water-melon.

" If you do that again I shall leave the room," she said.

" Do what?"

" Yawn. Can't you eat your yawns? It shows very little strength of will if you cannot. The ugliest thing in the world is one of those griffins with a great gaping mouth that supports shields, and after them the next ugliest thing is a man yawning."

" I beg your pardon," said Rannicar, rising and holding out his ·hand, " I will

not be the next ugliest thing in the world
again, for I am going to say good night.
Will you say good night to your mother
for me ?"

" My mother ! That is my aunt, not my
mother. If it had been my mother you
would not be now going home bored and
yawning."

" Should I not ?" said Ranicar, lingering.
" Is she so beautiful then ?"

" So people say."

" In that dimly - lighted hurly - burly
next door, beauty might as well be
ugliness."

" It was not dark at first. You could
see that Miss or Mrs. Medium was handsome ?"

" Yes ; I saw that."

" Then you do think her beautiful ?"
said Susie, sharply.

"Yes; a spit-fire, gipsy beauty. Softening a little, perhaps, under the influence of my friend Eugene's suave tones."

"They had met before," said Susie.

"Why do you think so?"

"I saw it in her red-hot eyes."

"*You* had met Everard before?"

"Twice; down in the Isle of Wight. Come," she cried, impulsively, "let us go back and be bewitched."

"Befooled, rather."

"Then befooled. I find it tame in here, in the light, with a yawning you; come back into the manufactured twilight, and let us be befooled together. It is better and more amusing for you, be sure, than going home to bed."

"Who is to befool me?"

"She will."

"No; because it is her trade. But

come ; let us go and try again to be enter-
tained by bad jugglery."

They went back to the confused darkness of the next room. Susie, creeping up
to one of the lamps, turned it broadly into
a full light. For an instant confusion was
confounded. Léontine cast a glance of
fury at her. Susie gave a little childish
laugh. The light revealed Eugene still
sitting beside the medium. There was a
burning colour in Léontine's dark cheeks,
and a passionate pleasure in her eyes.
Eugene seemed absorbed in watching her.
Susie thought he would never look away.
When he did, it was to glance, not at
Alice, but at her own little pale face. His
expression changed ; he got up and went
over to where she was sitting. " I took
your place," he said, bending over her ;
" do you want it again ?"

" No ; *indeed* I do not," answered Susie, emphatically ; " I'd rather sit and hold a bat or a snake than her hand. What is her name ?"

" Miss Léontine Médor."

" Have you ever seen her before ?"

" Once. How is your dog ?"

" You need not have been in such a hurry to change the conversation ; I was not going to ask you any more questions. He is very well, thanks. So is Alice's dog Charlie, that you gave her."

" Oh ! A pretty little fellow, isn't he ?"

" So pretty that he is made a bone of contention of from morning till night. No, from morning till morning ; for the children quarrel about which shall have him to sleep with them !"

" Do they quarrel over him ?"

" Indeed they do. Sometimes I actually
think that I shall see Cora staggering back
against the wall with his head and
shoulders, and Lucy capsizing into the
coal-scuttle with his tail and hind-legs.
Oh, Mr. Hungerford!" as that gentleman
came near her, " are you made a believer
in it ? Shall you ever come again and sit
hand in hand in the dark ?"

" Yes ; I think I shall."

" Then you are interested in it?"

"Not particularly; but I shall come
again nevertheless. Good night."

CHAPTER VIII.

PALMISTRY.

MR. VAN VLECK intended that Léontine should be a maker of the almighty dollar.

A little back room in Swanbury Crescent was made gorgeous and Oriental for her. She was advertised as a " Trance, test, and clairvoyant medium ; for revealing startling facts ; to be consulted on affairs connected with the living and dead. Hours, 12 till 8. Terms, one guinea."

In her brilliant room, astounding in its

colours, its furniture, its whole aspect, she looked a thrilling thing. Hearts beat faster, lips trembled, clear understandings grew muddled, sharp eyes became dull, when the owners of the same stood on the inside of those noiselessly swinging velvet doors, and found themselves face to face with eyes that no plummet of searching gaze could ever fathom.

Wonderful indeed they thought her. Startling were the revelations she made, discomposing the disclosures. She was strong in some occult force which they were wanting in ; where they were stone blind, she saw ; where their thoughts wandered gropingly, hers followed unerringly. She was young, beautiful, and a woman. The guineas poured in fast.

One afternoon, just as the daylight was beginning to die out, she sat alone at last,

after a day of hard work. A startled
gentleman, who had come incredulous, and
gone away convinced, had just been shown
out. She threw herself down on a low,
broad couch, firelight making one cheek
red, moribund daylight making the other
pale. The doors which she had not thought
to see open again to-night, swung open now.
A man's figure entered, and advanced towards her. She stopped playing with the
seed-pearl fringe of a silken covering which
Mr. Van Vleck had brought from the Le-
vant, and the daylight-tinted cheek grew
firelight-tinted. The man was Mr. Everard.

"Will you look into my unknown
future, and tell me something of it?" he
asked.

Her breathing grew quicker.

"Sit down in front of me," she answered,

"and hold out your hand. I must look into your hand to tell you of the future; the past and present I read through your eyes."

Eugene took his place in front of her, and near enough for her to take easily the hand he extended to her.

She folded her arms, and bending her head, looked with a brow-knit eagerness into the upheld palm; so closely and eagerly, that he felt the warm breath on his sensitive palm nerves.

She was quite silent, and for so long a time that he grew impatient.

"Come," he said, "are you going to tell me what you see in my hand? Do you see weal or woe, success or failure, long life or short?"

She looked up at him with the sunny smile that only a daughter of the south can have.

"I shall keep this knowledge for my-self," she said. "You must not give your guinea. I will read you as easily as if you were a sign-board; but I shall not tell you what it is I read. I shall not tell any one. I shall keep it to myself; it shall be my own, own possession," and she laughed.

Eugene drew back his hand hastily.

"That requires my permission," he said, haughtily.

She fastened her eyes greedily on his face.

"Too late," she said. "I read you like an open book."

"Or pretend that you do," he mut-tered.

"I read you like an open book," she repeated. "You have marked, and will mark, many heart lines——"

She paused.

" Surely," he said, in his low, memorable voice, " after coming here full of the deepest interest and curiosity, you will not send me away unsatisfied ?"

" Yes, I shall," returned she, darting a glance at him, fraught with sorcery.

There was nothing in her face that forbade his approaching his own more closely to it ; there was nothing in her eyes that repelled an ardent glance from his own into them ; there was nothing in her low, tremulous voice to discourage him from sinking his own to a dulcet monotone.

The bright blaze leaping up, made wells of fire of her dark eyes. There was something about her uncanny, yet ensnaring. In her presence, Eugene felt like a naked human soul, without appanages of Norman blood, aquiline features, patrician length of limb, and those more remote accessories of wealth, rank and position, and he had never been able to forget them before.

" You are not angry with me for refusing to tell you what I suppose I had no right to withhold from you?" asked Léontine, her eyes seeming to lengthen, soften, darken, as they shared the smile which displayed her glittering teeth.

"Yes—no," answered the man of the world, with rustic hesitation.

Thanks were spoken, thanks were smiled, thanks were looked by Léontine. A flimsy veil of gratitude, from behind which peeped out a beautiful and resolute woman's determination to be loved.

The daylight died quite away, and still Eugene stayed. Some one came in softly, and placed candles on the table, but still he lingered on. When at last his sense of the proprieties dragged his other charmed and unwilling senses away, the shivering stars were up in the cold November sky, the street lamps were lit, and night was closing in.

CHAPTER IX.

A GNAT MAY TROUBLE A LION.

AS Ranicar Hungerford was walking in the Park a few days after the séance, his attention was attracted to a deplorable object, hatted, habited, and mounted on a sedate grey horse. Deplorable because its face was so white and scared, its eyes so terrified, its lips so pale and trembling. It was Susie, taking her first ride in the Park. A steady old groom rode on one side of her; on the other, Alice, her blue eyes full of a tranquil enjoyment of her cousin's sufferings—an enjoyment which she did not allow her lips to express.

Ranicar leaned over the rail and put up his glass.

"Don't they see that the child is almost fainting?" he said to himself, compassion creeping into his heart.

As they came up to him, Susie, whiter than the cliffs of Dover, swayed in her saddle; Alice, staring hard at *him*, observed her not; the old groom, less absorbed in self and handsome lounger, came to a standstill, laying his hand at the same time on the bridle of Susie's horse, and checking it too.

Alice looked sharply, crossly round, and gave a little scream. Ranicar, hastily slipping under the rail, caught Susie in his arms just as she swayed over, the whip dropping from her little limp hand, her foot still in the stirrup; this he extricated.

As she opened her eyes immediately, Alice did not get down, contenting herself with asking Mr. Hungerford plaintively what was to be done.

"I can tell you very quickly," he answered. "You go on with your ride, and I will take your cousin home in a cab. You feel like yourself again, don't you, and able to go?"—this to Susie.

"Perhaps I had better come, too," said Alice, suddenly tending towards Samaritanism.

"Not the least use; a pity to spoil your ride. Besides, I am constitutionally opposed to four-wheelers. I will take Miss Dawnay with great care, believe me, in a hansom."

Alice's vanity being rasped, and her inclination thwarted, she made her ill-natured eyebrows nearly stand on end, dropped her eyelids, grew pink, and muttered something about " Mamma thinking it odd."

But Susie suddenly spoke up faintly, yet with spirit.

" *My* mother would have no objection to my going with such an *elderly* and *respectable* person." There she paused for breath, and a slight mischievous laugh. " If you had not kept me awake till four this morning, telling me hobgoblin stories, Alice," she went on, " this would not have happened. I am not such a contemptible muff as your face remarks that I am. Ta-ta, go on with your ride; I would not spoil it for the world. Kindness is not the word for this, Mr. Hungerford——"

Sick and dizzy again, she stopped. He drew her arm through his, and walked her away to the Albert Gate, lifting his hat in farewell to Alice. Alice rode on without turning to look after them.

To be called "elderly" and "respectable," even in half jest, was a new sensation to Ranicar. He felt as if he were being looked at through the wrong end of an opera-glass.

"Wretched to be a faggot of nerves, is it not?" he asked coldly and slightly, as they took their seats in the hansom.

"I don't know, I'm sure," said Susie. "I am not nervous, as a rule; only certain things make me nervous. Disagreeable, ill-proved things, with a downward tendency, make me so. Things that convince the judgment, and sweep the ground from under your feet, have not the same effect; but things that put worrying thoughts into the head, for which the person who gives

them provides no answer, I confess *do* make
me nervous. I give you an instance. Some
articles called ' Vagaries,' that came out in
the---"

" Ha !" ejaculated Ranicar, leaning his
elbows on the door of the hansom; " do
you know who wrote them ?"

" Y—yes," said Susie, knowing that she
was going to prevaricate, and feeling quite
unhappy in contemplating her wickedness
—" I have heard his name, but I've—I've
forgotten it. The writer was described to
me, too."

" Was he ? What was the description ?
I know the man slightly. Was he described
as an elderly and respectable person ?"

" He—let me see—he was described as
being not *at all handsome,*—as having eyes
the colour of a thunder-cloud, looking as if
he had a tooth-ache (having a tooth-ache

and being very much bored, give a face the same expression, you know), and wearing rings on his singularly tale-telling hands that had once been worn by dead relations."

Ranicar gave a short dry laugh. "What are tale-telling hands, pray?"

"I mean that they look——" quite forgetting herself; then catching herself up again—"I don't know what the person who told me meant."

"Ask them, will you?" said Ranicar carelessly.

But Susie, with a conscience-smitten look, did not answer him. "I am like the dropped stitch in a stocking, without Méry!" she exclaimed. "I go ravel, ravel, ravelling down, and am not able to help it. I need her to pick me up again."

A dissatisfied expression settled on her

face.   If he had been an old umbrella-
mender, with a plurality of hats, she could
not have looked at him with more coldly
unappreciative eyes ; but he was so peculiarly constituted that this served the turn
of Eros as no artless or studied flattery, no
skilled or guileless glances of admiration at
his handsome face could have done.   She
had lain for an instant a helpless child in
his arms, too, and he had been inspired
with a transient pity for her.   Small things,
these ; but small things are often the initia-
tion of events grotesquely disproportioned
to their littleness.

The words those curling, naïf lips uttered,
seemed to him to be something that he had
been waiting for years to hear.   So many
women had talked *at* him, dressed at him,
smiled at him, been lovely mute beggars for
his name and position.   Here was a little,

cool, pale girl who talked *to* him, partially saw through him, looked away from him, and seemed almost ready to see a ludicrous side to his character. He felt a pleasurable emotion as he made full and free acquaintance with every tint and line of Susie's unveiled youthful face. There was so little self-consciousness in her that she actually seemed to forget she had a face, which was a refreshing change to him, after studying the features of women who tried to make their expression subserve their interests.

Words that he thought must be agreeable to her, or any other woman, coming from him, rose to his lips, but died there, as he watched the frank young countenance translating some message from the heart.

Eugene Everard was walking slowly along the pavement, and she was looking at

him,—that was all, but it was everything.

" I want him to see me !" she said, under
her breath.

"Do you? Why?" returned Ranicar,
coldly, catching what she said.

" I want him to wonder—"

" Wonder at what ?"

Susie only blushed eloquently, for Eugene
was taking off his hat, and she was bowing
back to him with a shy smile.

Under the soft sky of Mentone lay
Ranicar's only sister in her quiet grave.
Two years ago she had died. People had
hinted that if there were such a thing as
a broken heart, that heart of hers, now
mouldering, was broken.

Opposite her bed, the bed on which she
died, had used to hang the picture of some
one dressed in Rifle-green. In one corner

two little letters were scrawled—E. E. they were. When she died, the picture was turned towards the wall first; then a man's jewelled hand detached it; and the same hand, trembling with fury, drove a knife-blade through the azure-eyed, smiling face, and flung it savagely into a blazing fire.

" He has on uniform !—oh !" said Susie.

" Do you find a man in a peculiarly dark volunteer uniform such a dazzling apparition ?"

" No," said Susie, loftily, "but I like a uniform."

"And what about the man in that uniform ? Do you find him to your taste ?"

"Oh, yes," answered Susie, speaking somewhat carelessly, but not as much so as she desired, " he is nice enough." *Too* careless these four last words. Suspiciously careless enough to make Ranicar draw his lips into a thin, hard line under his moustache.

"This has been too good of you," said Susie, touching his hand lightly as she jumped out, for they were now at the door. Ranicar rather wished that Mrs. Willis lived at Fulham. "*Too* good. Will you come in? I'll thank you some more if you will come in where there are no cabmen."

"You tempt me very much, but I cannot, thanks. You will see me to-morrow night, for your aunt wrote me a note, saying there was to be a séance, and I am coming to it."

"Oh, are you? Well, *au revoir* then. I did not *faint*, remember."

Then she ran up the steps with an

abruptness that bordered on incivility, and was gone.

But Ranicar was rather tired of good manners.

CHAPTER X.

THE ART OF CONVERSATION, ACCORDING TO SUSIE.

 WOMAN is true to her best instincts when she avoids the blurting candour of wounding truthfulness, and cleaves to the tender deception of assuaging evasions.

Susie was generally true to her second best instincts, and was candid where candour was sure to annoy, displease, and hurt. Her small prevarication of yesterday made her a prey to remorse until the moment when she found Ranicar seated beside her, and clasping her hand in the mystic circle, and was able to whisper to him without preamble, " It was *you* who 'wrote those things in the ——, and nobody described you to me. I looked at you, and said what I did, just for mischief."

His face changed. She had purposely made him an object of ridicule, then ! It would not do to allow her to know that he had actually believed she was only repeating some one else's words.

" Of course," he said, in a very low, calm voice. " Is it possible that you thought I had any vanity to wound ? or even if I had, that *you* could wound it ?"

" I thought you might have," said Susie, speaking louder in her earnestness, " because I know that it only needs for a man to be a very little bit good-looking, and he is vain."

"What sort of men can you have met, poor child?"

"All sorts," said Susie, hastily.

"Sh! Sh!" came from some one opposite. Susie fancied from Mr. Everard. Ranicar knew it.

Eugene, who always hankered after that which another desired, and seemed working to possess, found in Hungerford's roused manner in speaking to Susie, and his self-forgetful glances towards her, direct testimony to Susie's claim on his own interest.

Accordingly, when the circle was broken, and the lamps bright, he went over to her side.

"You and Hungerford seemed to have hit on something very interesting to talk about."

Ranicar, who still lingered by her, looked away carelessly and indifferently, listening absorbedly.

"Not in the least interesting," said
Susie, disclaiming eagerly. "Not a bit.
I was wondering, so was Alice, whether you
would come to-night. Are they going to
make a convert of you? Oh, Mr. Everard,
don't let them."

"There is no fear of it; perhaps if every
one I found here were enthusiastic on the
subject, I should be swayed—"

"Almost every one that you find here
does believe in it; *I* don't."

"No, *you* don't."

Ranicar moved away, bitten by his snake-
ring, so hard-clenched was the hand which
wore it.

"*You* don't, and you a believer and an
enthusiast, I should find very convincing."

"No, no!" said Susie, movingly. "If
the beautiful medium does not convince you,
how could I?"

" She convinces me of one or two things,
but not of the truth and credibility of
Spiritualism.   You, too, convince me of one
or two things."

" Oh, what are they ?   Tell me ! tell
me !"

" I had begun to doubt that there were
any such things left in the world as honesty
and ingenuousness, and the frankness of
childhood lingering after childhood had
passed ; but when I saw you, the doubt
was dispelled.   I really believe you are
exactly what you appear to be."

" Of course I am."

" That when you seem to be pleased, you
are pleased ; when you seem to be sulky, it
is because you *are* sulky, not because you
put on a pout, and lower your eyelids,
fancying that it makes you look like a
Greuze, or a something or other you have

seen in a gallery, and fondly imagined was like you."

" I should never imagine myself like a Greuze or anything else," said Susie, bursting into a self-derisive laugh. " Strange that a person who is not sincere should value sincerity," she went on.

" But you do not think that I am insincere ?"

" I do not think that sincerity is ever so sweet-spoken as you are. Look at *me*—" (Eugene looked and laughed. She frowned back at him for this too literal interpretation of her words). " Look at me," she repeated. " Why, I all but tell people exactly what I think of them, and how they do hate me ! I have been so young up to now, that I have only been an *enfant terrible;* but fancy an *enfant terrible* grown up, and that is what I shall be, if I don't

take care. But I am going to correct myself. You can't go through life, you know,
saying what you think."

"I should, if I were you. It is admirable
to be so candid."

"I'd rather be sweet than candid," said
Susie, and was not ashamed to roar with
laughter at her own small fun, and wondered
why *he* did not laugh more. She had not
learnt that people laugh louder when you
do *not* laugh.

"They are already beginning to think,"
said she—"I mean Aunt Adria, and Alice,
and Uncle Willis—that I am a most disagreeable inmate, and Mr. Hungerford re-
warded me just now for my truthfulness
by a snub—at least it was going to be a
snub, it was just coming out of the shell—
when you said, 'Hush!' So you see my
popularity is as great as ever up here!"

"Do tell me what you were saying to him," said Eugene, eagerly.

Susie shook her head.

"Yes, pray do, I—"

"Mamma has a set of signals for me," continued Susie, cleaving his sentence in half without compunction. "She always has one ear open for me, no matter who she is talking to; and I have learnt to understand the flicker of an eyelash, the most imperceptible nod, coming from *her*; but now you see, I am as independent as a —as a comet."

"But your aunt—" began Eugene.

"Oh, but I scarcely see her all day."

"How do you know what I was going to say?" said Eugene, with perfectly unruffled temper. "You didn't let me finish my sentence."

"Oh, I knew exactly what you were

going to say," said Susie, carelessly. "I
should like to cut everybody's sentences in
half; I always know what they mean before they've finished, so it is just as well to
economize their words for them. People do
talk so much on a stretch."

"They ought to take a hint from *you*,"
said Eugene, with playful irony.

"There! I wish I had never allowed
you to finish that speech," said Susie. "I
did hope that I had at last found somebody
who would be amiable to me. For you
have been, until now. I shall never forget
how sweet you were down at home. Just
a little mawkish, you know, but *flawlessly*
amiable, unmixedly sugary. Now what *I*
should like to be, is an extremely fascinating
person who tells the truth. Mamma says that
I have no adaptability. A pretty long word,
isn't it? That is exactly what you *have?*"

"According to that, then, we are counter-parts," said Eugene. "I expect to see you in a year or two a mild, evasive lady, saying the right thing to everybody, and very easy to get on with."

"There is an old gentleman who lives down near us, who plants walking-sticks and umbrellas, and expects them to *grow*," returned Susie. "Yes, really; he waters them with the kindest care, loosens the earth round their tender ferules, watches them as a mother her sick child, tries one after another, still hoping for success. He has quite a large bed of them.—But don't you know him? You must be quite a home in our neighbourhood."

"I am," said Eugene, "but I have only the merest——"

"But you *took* me?" asked Susie earnestly, not observing that he had coloured, and shifted his glance away from her uneasily in replying.

" You see what I mean ? That you both expect impossibilities ?"

" Yes ; he is mad, of course——"

" Now that I think of it, ours is a rather mad neighbourhood."

" Look here, you are getting personal. My uncle is a neighbour of yours ; *I* sometimes am."

Eugene had risen, and with his patience just a little overtaxed was looking about the room. There stood Leontine talking to Mrs. Willis. What about, he wondered? Progression? Causal force — could there be a more Phidian head than hers ? More exact features, more smiting eyes ?

Susie had followed the direction of his eyes with her own.

"I should like to tell her," she said, "just what a humbug I consider her?"

"I should like to tell her——"

"Just what a beauty you consider her?"

"Very well, yes. It is quite as well to let you finish my remarks in your own way, as you will not let me finish them in my own."

Here a young lady began to sing; or rather, having seated herself at the piano, she began to play an accompaniment to words distinctly spoken in a faint, doleful sort of recitative.

"Do you know what I call *that?*" asked Susie, in a round, unsoftened voice. "I call it 'Words without Songs.'" And she laughed with the greatest relish.

"You will go and tell her so, *of course?*"

"Why of course?"

"That is your way, is it not? I have

gathered as much from what you have said."

Susie paused to think.

" No, no," she said, putting her head on one side, and considering. "That is a little *too* much of the monkey you know."

" I wish I could get you to tell me what you said to——"

" He looks like a picture of an old knight —or rather an old picture of a knight, doesn't he ?—standing there ?"

Eugene found. that the only way to manage was to disregard her. "To Hungerford ?—And by the way, what were you doing with him yesterday in a hansom, and with a riding-habit on ? Are you fast ? That was a fast thing to do."

" Funny! he actually took the trouble to ask me yesterday what I thought of *you,* and here you are thinking it worth while to

ask me my opinion of him! Circumstances
over which one has no control placed me in
that hansom with him; and as for being
fast it was the slowest thing I ever did in
my life."

"Really? Slow? I thought he banished every feeling, but pleasure and
triumph. Pleasure at his wit and wisdom,
triumph at having been able to place
yourself under their influence."

"Now it is my turn to say, Really?
I could not have been worthy of having
everything banished but this, for I felt much
as usual. I was too insignificant you see."

"World-worn men often fancy just such
naïve, fresh children as you. As nothing
can ever surprise, or please, or amuse them
very much, they like something that it is
possible to surprise, delight, and amuse
twenty times a day."

" Don't," said Susie, frowning. "I don't like to hear you talk so."

" Susie," said the chill voice of Mrs. Willis, " come here, my dear ; we wish to hear you sing."

Susie, frowningly going forward, was about to refuse, when Eugene's earnest voice begging for "one song," as a famished man might beg for bread, turned the scowling negative into a reluctant affirmative.

Alice feeling terribly interfered with, and looking pouting and sulky, sat with only the companionship of a very angry mood. Hungerford stood opposite the folding doors with an immobility of feature that tells suspiciously nothing.

" You are going to sing," he said, coming towards Susie, " I wish it was to me only !"

Susie gave a startled look up at him ; he thought it the sweetest look that he had ever seen on a woman's face. When he heard her voice he found that it possessed the rare quality which prevented it from reminding one of the voice in speaking. It had not too human a sound. It was flute-like, bell-like, bird-like by turns, but it never for one instant sounded like Susie's voice in speaking.

"You are she," he said to himself,

"In whose least act abides the nameless charm
That none else has for me."

CHAPTER XI.

A PEEP AT THE WILLIS FAMILY.

SUSIE found that as a sojourning place for the soul, her aunt's house might be all that was elevating, cultivating, educating, refining ; but as an abiding place for the body, it was just a little confused, disjointed, disorderly, unlooked after.

It is ten o'clock of a snapping January morning. A busy, nipping wind is making weepy eyes, violet cheeks, blue noses ; painting the human face with hideous war-paint, to do battle with it; sending stray bits of paper on swift, aimless errands, despatching scattered rubbish on dirty missions to freshly scoured areas.

Susie, who has always been an early riser, has breakfasted tête-à-tête with her uncle. Now he has gone money-grubbing in the city. Susie runs to the window and watches him depart. He is going by the underground railway, and sets off for the station on foot.

She nods and smiles at him as he goes by, but he does not see her; tramping past without looking up, only buffeting with the wind.

It is always a foolish feeling to speak to some one who does not hear, to nod and smile at some one who is totally unconscious of these our muscular tokens of goodwill.

"He did not see me," says Susie, turning and speaking apologetically to the
furniture.

How still the house is, but for a faint,
mysterious, scraping, scratching sound from
the hall.

There are no signs of Alice. Mrs. Willis
has breakfasted in her dressing-room, as
she usually does. Susie looks at the clock,
turns her glance to the breakfast-table.

The empty egg - shells, jam - smeared
plates, bacon gradually changing its hot
transparency to cold opacity, give her a
feeling of repletion.

" Doomed never to be a chicken!" she
says, driving the spoon still more firmly
through the empty egg-shell, and making
it stand upright.

Then she yawns and goes out of the
room, leaving the door open.

The peculiar fidgeting, *crawly* sound is explained on going into the hall, by finding Lucy sliding down the baluster with an air of inexhaustible enjoyment.

"Where's Miss Wix, Lucy? I am longing for a walk. Have you been? or are you going?"

"I don't know," says Lucy; "Miss Wix is writing something for mamma. Our lessons are put off till she's finished."

"And where is Harriet?"

"Upstairs mending our stockings," answers Lucy, editorially, and slides down with shrieks of friction.

Susie mounts upwards, and hearing the sound of a voice in the drawing-room, looks in. Cora is in possession. She has braided her fair hair into two ragged pig-tails, and fastened the ends of them on the top of her head with a high Spanish comb.

She has purloined one of Alice's smart little aprons, and helped herself out of a cabinet of curiosities to a string of amber beads, wherewith to adorn her neck. She has also made herself a train, by fastening a waterproof cloak round her waist by the neck; the hood turned inside out makes a pannier like a plum-pudding, and is very satisfactory.

She is kneeling on the hearth-rug combing Charlie, who, with short irritated yelps, tries to get away, snapping first over one shoulder, then over the other. As he all but succeeds in making off, she combs him back again. She is talking to him all the time.

Susie stops to listen.

"My young May Moon, but you must be combed. Sugar-plum dog, be quiet! Sweet as sugar that grows on a tree!

Bright being from another sphere! If you'll be good, we'll take you all to walk with us. Yes, all of you, from your nose to your tail. You imp of darkness! You nearly bit me!"

" Oh! you little—coxcomb—you little fop! (Where *is* the word I want!) What are you doing?" says Susie, entering.

" I am not a cock's-comb," replies Cora, starting to her feet, and getting as red as that crown of the poultry-yard potentate which she mentions.

" I never saw anything so ridiculous in my life," continues Susie, gazing at the waterproof cloak, the Spanish comb, the beads, and the apron.

It is astonishing what a stock of abusive words children have. Susie is now treated to some of the most trenchant in her cousin's vocabulary. She winds up by saying that Susie is a "nasty beast of a meddler."

Susie makes her escape and goes on to her intended *gîte*, Alice's room. She opens the door unceremoniously and walks in. Alice is "*happed*" up in bed, the window-curtain drawn aside to admit just a shaft of light that falls on the novel she holds.

The room is rather cold, but her face is crimsoned with the excitement of the scene she is reading. It is a French novel, of accurate immoralities.

She starts as Susie enters, saying, impatiently :—

" Well ?"

" Oh, are you not up ?" says Susie, in a tone nicely balanced between surprise and disgust.

" You see that I am not."

" But why ain't you ? Mr. Mon Santo

12—2

will be here at eleven, and it is half-past ten now."

" I can't take my singing lesson possibly; I have an *affreux* headache !" replies Alice, raising her eyebrows, dropping her eyelids, and feeling exactly like Mme. De Fange, who always breakfasts in bed surrounded by all that there is of the most marvellously beautiful in art and upholstery, her chocolate in a *faïençe* cup, handed her by the intrigue-assisting femme-de-chambre.

" You look as if you had," replies Susie, staring with obvious disapproval at her cousin. " If you were blushing for the sins of the whole human family you could, not have a redder face."

Alice, who is feeling *raffinée, frêle, pleine d'une sympathique amenité*, all like Mme. De Fange, is roused into acerbity of speech.

She requests Susie, with some warmth, to leave the room.

Susie does so, and after standing for a moment, ruffled, lonely, and at a loss, resolves to penetrate to her aunt's dressing-room.

She finds Miss Wix there, seated at the window, writing; her little rabbit profile unassisted to a definite outline by the strong, sharp light behind it.

Mrs. Willis, in a pretty dressing-gown trimmed with lace, is writing, too. She hands over her rough, rapid jottings to Miss Wix, who copies, smooths, arranges.

" Well, Susie ?"

" The fact is, Aunt Adria, that I'm longing to go out," says Susie, apparently beginning in the middle of a sentence, " or I would not have come in and disturbed you. Could I not run out for

a few minutes by myself, for a mouth-
ful of fresh air, before Mr. Mon Santo
comes ?"

" By no means," answers Mrs. Willis,
hazily. " By no means. After Miss Wix
has finished writing for me, you can go
with her and the children ; there will be
time before luncheon. They need not to-
day have lessons until afterwards."

" Could *I* write anything for you, Aunt
Adria ? I write quickly. My m's and n's
and u's are all shaped like spear-heads, but
they are pretty legible."

" I wish," said Mrs. Willis, with sudden
earnestness, " that young people could be
made to think less of the fleeting present
and more of the never-ending future. I
wish they could be brought to see what the
true aims of life are."

" Mother has taught me," said Susie,

simply—"at least, she has taught me. to know what they are, even if I do not succeed in practising them."

"Young people," continued Mrs. Willis, pursuing her own train of thought, "live as if this life was all. Do they realize what it would be if it *were* all ? What a mockery, what a spirit-breaking encounter with circumstance, what a dying by inches, only to *die !*"

Mrs. Willis's voice broke down, her lips grew white. Like many others, she had found the thought of uncertainty as to a future state so insupportable, that, craving fuller assurance than what is given in the simply solemn words of the Bible, she had feverishly seized at what seemed like tangible proof of the thing she thirsted to know. She was no happier than before. The black doubt still dogged her; and still she watched

and hungered and sought for surer signs;
but never to have the peaceful faith of her
early womanhood again—ah! never again.
There is no peace in trying to replace faith
by *sight*.   There would have been peace
could she only have meekly resigned herself
to feeling—"I shall be satisfied; but, oh!
not *here*."

"Do *you* realize what it would be, Susie,
for this life to be *all*?"

Susie shuddered from head to foot.

"Of course," she said.   "Anything that
has been something does not want to be
nothing!   Fearful! Oh, Aunt Adria, don't
don't make me think of it!"

Little Miss Wix, her eyes vacantly fixed
on the wall, bites the tip of her pen and
does a mental sum.

"Anything that has been something does
not want to be nothing."

She stops biting her pen and meditates. The mental arithmetic is suspended.

Well, yes; even a something that has been only a little plodding, poorly-paid nursery-governess would rather go fagging on for an unlimited number of years, an insignificant joyless anything, than be—*nothing.*

"Immortality!" says Mrs. Willis, clasping her hands till the tendons stand out from the strain put upon them. "August, thrilling word! And are we to loose you from our warm human grasp, to give you over to the cold, hard uses of chiselled marble, and fading picture, and mouldering paper? Oh! the Inquisitors of other days, who tortured the body and allowed that there was a soul to curse, were merciful compared with these men, who, seated on crumbling intellectual heights, wring the

heart by dogmatic denial and emphatic
doubt."

She stops, looks at Susie's attentive,
honest face. Susie, young, trusting, en-
viably unshaken — Susie, who had been
taught the simple old faith, and who, perhaps—happy Susie!—may cling to it with
childlike confidence all her life.

> "'The world is something, none can doubt,
> But no one finds the secret out;
> To childhood, and to souls devout,
> Comes the best revealing,'"

murmurs Mrs. Willis. "Miss Wix, I think
that you need not write any more at present. Go and take Miss Cora and Lucy for
a walk. Go with them, Susie, since you are
longing for fresh air."

CHAPTER XII.

HUNGERFORD IN SUSPENSE.

S if seized with the most absorbed
credulity, or the most pains-
taking spirit of inquiry, Hungerford from this time made his appearance
at everything spiritualistic that included
little Miss Dawnay. Very often, too, he
joined her in her rides.

Sometimes, imprecating Eugene Everard,
he told himself that he had everything to
fear from him, as he watched the faint
colour going and coming in Susie's cheeks

when Eugene was talking to her in his un-
meaningly devotional way. At other times,
metaphorically snapping his fingers in Everard's face, he would assure himself that
there was nothing to fear from him, as he
noted the look of cold disgust on Susie's
face when some decipherable glance of pas-
sion passed between him and the Creole.

Once—one night after walking miles up
and down the room, and after receiving
much electricity from the carpet—he seemed
to recover those sensations which had been
his before Susie had proved to him that
the formidable foe to his indifference was
indifference.

Coming to a standstill, he looked into his
own face in the glass, and felt that from
that moment he abjured the pale-faced,
blunt, and difficult child who had wound
herself about his heart.   He dwelt with

sturdy determination on the irregularity of
her white features, on the crudity of her
manners, on all her bars to beauty and fascination. That he, of all men, should ad-
mire that which was not admirable—should
be captivated by what was not charming !

He threw his whole will-power into the
effort to convince himself that from this
moment he was a free man again. Free to
criticize unlovingly, free to judge with cold
nicety, free to cavil unsparingly as he had
once done.

Full of the fine sense of self-mastery and
conviction, he betook himself to bed, only
to toss and turn sleeplessly ; his self-con-
gratulations and belief in his own self-
conquest seeming to drive everything like
repose away. He heard the clock in the
neighbouring steeple strike four times.
Four o'clock came of a cold winter's morn-

ing, and not for one instant had come to him the mild divider of what would otherwise be a maddening continuity of acts, words, and thoughts.

He was weary of his inward reasoning, and of his wakeful restlessness. Small vexations were no more bearable by him than a swarm of wasps by a tiger. He lighted the candle, and for a minute or two sat up, his chin resting on his hand, his brows knit, his eyes fixed as though weighing some intention in his mind, whose result might be momentous.

At last he put forth his hand and drew his watch towards him; a pen-knife, too, that lay on the table beside it. On his watch-chain hung as a charm a tiny Chinese trifle—a little blue porcelain tube, divided and hung in the middle by a gold ring. From one end of this tube he pricked a particle of some substance which he bit off the point of the blade. Then he flung down the watch and the open knife, extinguished the candle, and sank back on the pillow.

How was it that in all his tossings and turnings he had not been able to find this position before ? It was the position above all others that brought delicious ease to the limbs, rest to the head, relaxation to the muscles. In a few minutes slumber appeared to be pervading the chilly air he breathed ; a warm fragrance seemed to have usurped the cold and scentless atmosphere of his room, the clock in striking had lost its harsh distinctness, the five strokes sounded vague, far away, and musical. His thoughts, too, seemed to have lost their harsh distinctness, and were vague, and came to him, in a soft, rhythmical

monotony; then they became brightly
tinged and symmetrical, nothing that was
not pleasing being presented to the inner
vision.

Upon this followed a phase when, although grown more fascinating, more rosy,
they lost their just proportion, and were
the fantastic imageries not shaped by a
mind free from disturbing and unnatural
influences.

His limbs tingled slumberously, as though
every muscle were being touched with down
dipped in nard. Then an overpowering
drowsiness weighed on each stimulated
faculty; imagination, thought, and feeling
became merged in profound unconscious-
ness.

When he went to sleep it was six o'clock,
when he awoke it was eleven. His first
thought on opening his eyes was not of

Susie's imperfections, but of *Susie*, young and candid, fresh, pure, fair-faced, clear-eyed, silver-voiced, and enthrallingly indifferent to him. So much gained by the inner conflict between will and inclination of the night before.

At one o'clock he was riding by her side in a quiet part of the park, his heavy-lidded eyes fixed on her piquant face. Behind, with Alice, came Eugene Everard, only waiting his opportunity to slip into the place that seemed most desired by Hungerford. Alice, with her blooming face all aglow, was talking with the exhilaration of gratified vanity, skipping eagerly from one subject to another, because she only talked for talk's sake, and had no preference as regards topics. Very fragmentary and flighty talk it was, but she would have said that Eugene was delighted with it, for

he infused a misleading amount of attention and gratification into his face and
manner.

Mrs. Willis had by this time made so
many distinguished friends and acquaintances in the Spirit world, as to have almost
ceased to regard the claims of a rather
commonplace and undistinguished earthly
family.   More and more they were left to
the care of servants, governesses, and themselves.

The dress, deportment, etc., which she
had promised Mrs. Dawnay should be her
care, were neglected for higher demands on
her time, which took the varied shapes
that any dominant interest is sure to
assume.

"Your aunt tells me, Miss Dawnay,"
said Ranicar to Susie, "that she expects
to be in town until quite the end of

July. Shall you be with her all that time ?"

"I don't know. No, I think not. Mamma is probably coming up in April, and then I shall go into lodgings with her."

"I ask you," he said, in a low tone, " not because I am given to idle curiosity, but because my movements will be in some measure regulated by yours."

" Really ?" said Susie, who had caught the habit of using the word from her cousin, as young people do. " I should as soon imagine that you would give me your watch to regulate, as——"

She paused awkwardly.

" My giving you *myself* to regulate," he supplied, with a slight smile.

" Your movements," murmured Susie, " I was going to say that ; something about

your movements, I was going to say, you
know, but I had to stop and think what I
meant. Are you not very tired of London?
I thought people like you never stayed
in London in the winter—you and Mr.
Everard."

"It is very easy to see why Everard
stays," said Ranicar, trying not to speak
with a sneer.

"Why does he stay?" asked Susie,
eagerly.

Ranicar shrugged his shoulders.

"He stays to act the part of the biter
bit. He is bejuggled, bewitched."

"By the Creole," said Susie; not questioningly, but as an assertion.

He did not contradict her.

"He seems to like Alice," she continued,
timidly; "he is very often at the house
when Miss Médor is not there."

"He is almost a masculine personation of 'My last Duchess,' in that he 'loves whate'er he looks upon, and his looks go everywhere.'"

"I do not think you are right in that," said Susie, with a half sigh. "I am going to ask him," turning the sigh into a mischievous smile.

Ranicar frowned, and bit his lip ferociously, but before he could expostulate or prevent, Susie had turned her horse's head, and cut off Alice and Eugene as they came up.

"Mr. Hungerford says that you are like his last Duchess," she said, laughing lightly, "because you love whate'er you look upon."

"Does he say so?" answered Eugene, in a tone of threatening and formidable jocularity. "It is very flattering, Hungerford, that you should select me for a character-sketch." He pressed forward in speaking to Susie's side. Somehow Susie's horse, too, moved on. Ranicar and Alice were left abreast of one another. In the shape of small manœuvres nothing could have been more successful.

"What else did Hungerford say of me, pray?" asked Eugene.

"Nothing," answered Susie, becoming cautious and prudent, as she always was in speaking of people behind their backs, although those qualities were often conspicuously absent when she engaged in conversation *with* them.

"We are going to Mr. Van Vleck's to-night," she went on, partly to get away from the subject, partly to moot one of paramount interest to her. "There is to be an evocation of something or other; no-

body knows what, exactly. One or two
stubborn people, who have not been convinced before, are to be convinced to-night
by their own eyes. What would be the
long words for seeing with their own eyes?
I can't think of them."

" Ocular demonstration, I suppose."

" And you will be there, Mr. Everard?"

" Yes, I shall be there."

" You are infatuated with her."

" By no means," flushing hotly. " I am
interested in her."

Susie's truthful eyes were searching his.

" I am not a susceptible person. Believe
me, Miss Dawnay, when I say so, and
doubt Hungerford's misrepresentations if
they have led you to fancy the contrary."

" Oh, they have not; I am sure you are
not; but I see when you look at her that
your eyes and heart rebel against looking

anywhere else. She *is* beautiful; she is tropical, dark, fiery, the counterpart of a cold English nature."

He did not answer, and the look of hauteur that he could assume upon occasions settled on his face.

Susie, perceiving it, felt aggrieved, and pouted.

"Talk," she said, after a moment's unbroken silence. "Say something, do. I am tired of looking at your freezing face."

"Then why look at it?" he replied, smiling in spite of himself.

"I am not," staring between her horse's ears. "What was it I said that you did not like?"

"To tell you the truth, I sometimes object to personalities."

Susie looked deeply mortified. "I cannot bear being found fault with. I never could from a child," she said.

"*From* a child? Why, what are you now but the most engaging of children?" he rejoined, turning to her with his most cordial smile. It was not often that he lapsed from his sunny suavity as he had just done.

"I may have been a child when you first saw me, but I am not one now," she rejoined, with simple gravity.

"Have so many events been crowded into your life?"

"No, not that; but I seem to have found out so many new feelings, and so many new things about people."

"What new feelings have you found out, you fortunate discoverer?"

"Do not call me fortunate. I have discovered what it is to have an aversion; I have found out what it is—" She paused.

"Go on," he said, with some curiosity.

"I have found out what it is like," she continued, trying to speak in the same tone and manner that she had before used, "to think, and speak, and act for myself without having a mother to fly to for advice and dictation."

"Why have you taken an aversion to her?" asked Eugene, not very much heeding her last words, since they were not what he expected them to be.

"*Her!* you say *her* as if I had told you the name of the person."

"It is not hard to guess it."

"No, perhaps not for you to guess. I have a strong repugnance to her, because I think her an impostor. I detest deceit. But I'm not going to talk of her any more."

She touched up her horse, and went off at a trot. Eugene kept on at her side.

By this time Alice and Hungerford had cantered past them, and were seen going out of the gate. They followed.

"I can't help it," said Susie, as a revertive apology, "any more than I can help having an appetite. I do hope luncheon is ready. No, I'd rather Mr. Hungerford helped me down; he is a great deal taller than you are."

CHAPTER XIII.

A POPULAR SÉANCE.

ASTONISHING preparations for the evocation of the coming night were made in Swanbury Crescent. Not one of them savoured of the supernatural. A little room was separated from Léontine's room by a door of one great sheet of glass, and over it was a noiseless sliding panel papered like the rest of the room. There were, too, a few trifling arrangements as if for a celebration of the "Glorious 4th," and all was ready at eight o'clock.

Léontine moved about a dazzling apparition in black and gold and scarlet. She
was restless with impatience. She longed
to read in her uncle's face whether she was
looking her best to-night. There was a
little marplot and spoil-plan coming, who,
in Léontine's estimation, never had any
best. She was always pale and plain, with
a face as expressionless as a swan's egg.
Léontine was gazing at herself meanwhile
in one of the looking-glasses.

"I am not bad-looking, am I, Uncle
Aloysius?" she burst out at length.

"You're as handsome as they make 'em,"
answered he, succinctly.

"Here comes somebody!" cried Léontine,
starting away.

Enter a gentleman who had married first
a wife who was all body, secondly a spouse
who was all soul, and who now wanted
tidings from both of them.

It was tiresome, waiting for the people to file in. He for whom Léontine watched so feverishly was one of the last to come, and he entered the room by Susie's side. Susie looking up out of eyes as deep and honest as wells with truth lying at the bottom of them; Eugene bending his head with cordial courtesy to listen to what she was saying. Behind were the Willises and Mr. Hungerford.

"Are you going to frighten us very much to-night?" asked Eugene, with a smile, of Léontine. "I hear that you are."

"Yes, I hope so," she answered curtly, and drawing her eyebrows together.

"Don't do anything very terrible," he said, in a low voice, "for there is one very timid little heart here."

"Is it within my control? Timid hearts should not come here."

"I will sit beside her, and if she is frightened do my best to soothe her," said Eugene, watching carefully the effect of his words.

But Léontine was too complete and trained an actress to betray herself by any sign of feeling, and Eugene was sensible of a vague disappointment. He moved slowly away, and seated himself beside Susie.

There were the usual manifestations. Rather tame and used up they were by this time.

It was not until late that the event of the evening—the evocation—took place. Raps, spelt out beforehand, announced it to be Hendrick Hudson. And in the midst of rolling clouds of smoke and flickering gleams of pallid light, an indistinct form was visible for a few seconds, and then vanished, carrying with it much of the faith of those assembled, in Spiritualism ; for the Evocation was a failure. Everybody was so secretly or openly suspicious of trickery, of artifice, that there was a speedy breaking up, and a cool reluctance of manner, even on the part of the Spiritualist advocates, in admitting the supernatural claims of the apparition to credibility.

No arrangement was made with Mr. Van Vleck for a future séance; there was the censorious silence that tells so much, on all sides. People said good-night with an air of chill dignity, and departed.

"Shall you come to-morrow?" whispered Léontine to Eugene as he was taking leave of her (he had lingered until the last).

He fashioned a thought to suit himself, as we all can do on occasions.

"She is so beautiful; why should I not indulge an admiration which pleases and gratifies her, and is perfectly harmless—to myself, and very amusing. Yes," he said aloud, "I have some handwriting I wish you to characterize for me. About twelve I shall come."

This was only one of many times that he had made an excuse for coming by bringing scraps of handwriting for her to see.

When the doors had swung together after him, Mr. Van Vleck flung himself down in a chair in something the attitude of his national spread eagle, and dejection clouded his sharp, intelligent face.

" If we don't gain more headway, Leon, we must shut up shop," he said. " Folks are tired of the real genuine manifestations, levitation of ponderable objects, percussive sounds, music played by invisible agency and so on ; and if they are to be imposed on, I ain't the jockey to do it. I can't set up for a juggler ; I'm too old a dog to learn jugglers' tricks. Suppose you sink the medium, put the woman to the fore, make the most of your good looks, expend your will-power in fascination, and catch a landed proprietor."

" I don't know of one," said Léontine, in an even, unexpressive voice.

"I know of one *in posse,* don't you ? And by the time you've caught him he may be *in esse.* You know who I mean— Everard."

" Everard," repeated she, lingering over the name as if she liked hearing herself say it. " Yes, I might have known that you meant him——"

She could not meet her uncle's eyes, although she had self-mastery enough not to blush, or look confused.

" You shirk looking me in the face as

you answer," quoth he in a tone of quiet amusement. " So much the better ; I guess every female thing has her melting moments. Your heart would have done to ice a mint-julep with, Leon, but I shouldn't wonder if it was going to be thawed now."

To this Léontine gave no answer ; she made a movement impatient almost to fierceness.

" His old uncle, isn't it?" asked Mr. Van Vleck, after a pause.

" Isn't what?"

" His old uncle who is going to leave him the property. But I know it is. I only asked to draw you out. I might as well try, though, to draw a mouse out of a hole by showing it a cat ; 'tis his mother's brother, unmarried and elderly. Everard comes here too often for an indifferent man. He thinks he's amusing himself, perhaps.

14—2

It'll be a noble occupation for you, Léontine, to 'play the slave to gain the tyranny;' that is, if you succeed, and gain it. It won't be very noble if you fail. I've seen prosperous fortunes for two or three individuals made out of one young man's love folly. Gracious Peter! How love does dilute a man! Dilute him?" pausing to pile on contempt, "you could suck him through a straw!"

"A man must love very much," murmured Léontine, "to throw over barriers, and make light of objections many in number as the hairs of his head."

"But you'll do your best to make him, Léontine?" said he, rising.

"Yes, my very best," she murmured in a stifled voice.

"I say," he said, returning, "I should almost lot on it, if it wasn't for that little pale-faced thing. I'm afraid of her ways, and I'll bet you are, too. And I'll bet you don't love her, or you wouldn't have wanted to scare her so. For pure, gratuitous, unremunerative malice, give me a woman!"

" I should like," said Léontine, slowly, " to scr-ratch her with a rusty nail!"

CHAPTER XIV.

SUSIE ENGAGED.

OWARDS the end of the winter Mrs. Dawnay received a letter from Susie, which filled her heart with amazement, pleasure, pride. Ranicar Hungerford, of whom she had heard as being world-disdaining and world-beloved, fastidious, cold, and gently cynical, was attracted by her little daughter. From the elaborately evasive style of many of Susie's former letters she had suspected it. Now, as she read, the suspicion changed to certainty. She was conscious, too, that those short bald sentences expressed some misgiving, and implored counsel and help, although it was only in such words as these,—

"I almost wish I had not come up. I want to see you so much, and yet I hardly want to come back to forlorn Beaucome. Did you ever see Mr. Hungerford? He is handsome, is he not? and clever. A great deal cleverer than Mr. Everard. If we were rich, we should look at life through pink glass windows, shouldn't we? You don't believe in love nonsense, do you, mother? The best sort comes after marriage, doesn't it? Mr. Hungerford is so anxious to know you; he almost thinks of going down to the Isle of Wight on purpose to make your acquaintance. I think you would find that he spoke of me as if he

liked me very much. Do you remember
telling me once that the best way to make
people like one was to like people ? It is
an excellent rule ; I have tried it.

"If Mr. Hungerford should tell me still
more plainly than he has done how much
he likes me, guide me in what I am to say
to him. Suppose you sit down directly on
receiving this, and answer it."

Mrs. Dawnay did sit down directly and
answered it, writing with a most loving
heart certainly, but with a sufficiently cool
and judicious spirit guiding her pen.
Nothing was very emphatic that Mrs.
Dawnay said, but everything was written
with an intense desire to sway and convince.

Susie, on receiving the letter, ran up
to her own room with it, eagerly tearing
open the envelope as she went. After

reading it, she threw herself down on the bed, letter and all, and hiding her face in the pillow, burst into a fit of tears.

"Oh! mother, mother!" she whispered, "you are my guide, my ideal, and my trust. You and my own heart have never been at war before, but you and it are at war now!"

Susie was only seventeen, and her mental store was not great. She had no large fund of experience and self-knowledge to draw on. No stock of accumulated conclusions, or well-weighed probabilities. The words she said to herself were almost as simple as those Gretchen says as she pulls the daisy's pink-tipped petals.

"He loves me; *he* does not love me. *He*, not loving me, gives me only a heart-ache; self-contempt; I will forget him. Forget the tones of his voice, the expression of his face, the colour of his eyes—soon. Not all at once, but very soon." She started up and dried her eyes. " And I shall succeed in being rich and fine, and loved, too! Although I fail in being quite happy. But the great thing is to be loved."

She got off the bed and went to bathe the tear-marks from her face. Mingled with the splashing of the water, she heard her aunt's voice. Mrs. Willis had entered without knocking, and was speaking to her.

" Susie, Mr. Hungerford is in the drawing-room ; he is waiting to speak to you alone."

" Yes," said Susie, with the expression worn on seeing a letter with a black seal beside one's plate; " I've rather been expecting him."

"Ah!" returned Mrs. Willis; "then you are prepared to see him, and I need not make any comment on what I suppose lies before you."

Mrs. Willis spoke in the sleep-walker's tone that she had grown to have, absently twisting a bracelet round and round her wrist meanwhile. She glided on into her dressing-room, and Susie went slowly downstairs, thinking feeble thoughts of how it was what numbers of girls did; that mamma knew what was best. That nothing mattered so long as——

In the midst of the third thought she opened the drawing-room door and found herself face to face with Ranicar Hungerford.

She held out a hand to him in the half-way, slow manner of physical repulsion. He did not appear to notice, and grasped it strongly, seeming reluctant to let it go.

"I thought I should find you in," he said.

"The day is so stormy and wild that we have none of us been out," rejoined Susie. "Alice is in her room with a head-ache——"

"An undesirable companion," said Hungerford, filling in her pause, "a head-ache. Have you, too, a headache? There is a weary look about your eyes."

"No," replied Susie, selecting a small chair in an isolated position. "To tell the truth, I have been crying, and that is the reason my eyes look heavy and dull."

"Crying?" he repeated, tenderly. "Pray tell me what about."

"First one thing, then another; I began to cry over a letter from my mother;

then I found several other things to cry about, so I went on."

"Did your mother's letter so sadden you? But I will not annoy you with questions, although it is hard not to make your joys and sorrows my own ; would you be willing to let me share them with you —Susie ?"

Susie murmured something inarticulately, and slipping out of her seat, took up a position of armed neutrality at the piano.

"I did not hear," he said, following her.

Again she spoke, but this time her words were drowned in the soft and flute-like air she was playing.

He made the two small hands prisoners in one of his.

"You do not mean me to hear what you say," he cried, looking at her intently.

"In these strange evening meetings we have grown to know each other very well, have we not?" he went on abruptly.

"I do not feel that I know you very well," murmured Susie; "I can't tell how it may be with you; I daresay you may understand me; I must be a very simple story for you to read, you have such knowledge of the world and of character."

"And if I have, my knowledge has only taught me to distrust and to suspect. I have come to look upon human beings as motives—motives all tending self-ward. I cannot at this moment think of one person in the world who cares for me for my own sake. Since my sister died no one has prized me, I am bitterly conscious, except for the sake of what I could give them, get for them, help them to get. I have some prestige. Why, I know not; people value being seen with me, having me at their houses, having it known that I am their acquaintance; not for my own sake, but for the sake of what my advantageous worldly accidents have given me. This is very tiresome when it is all a man has. It is quite bearable, I dare say, when it is only a part of his life; when he has from one honest heart a love that is for himself alone; altogether apart from what fortune and circumstance have allotted to him. There is an honesty and a candour about you, little one, that drew me to you from the evening I first met you. I trust you; that does not surprise you, perhaps, for you probably know yourself to be trustworthy; and I love you."

Susie drew her hands away from his retaining ones, and let them rest slightly on the keys without sounding a note.

"Do you?" she said, very low. ."Why? I have not a pretty nor a charming face!"

"Your face is inexhaustible of charm to me," he replied, looking at her as Susie had once or twice in her life imagined a man looking, "and I love you—why, indeed! Because I believe that you were born for me to love."

"Expressly for the purpose!" said Susie, under her breath, with a little gleam of irritated amusement in her eyes.

"Yes," he said, catching her words, "expressly for the purpose. I have never loved any one before, as I do you. That is, I have never sincerely wished to make any one my wife, as I do you."

There was a pause.

"What is your answer; will you be my wife, or——"

Susie's answer was only to cower and

grow pale, and slide her fingers softly over the keys.

" Pray speak !" he said, in a low moved voice.

" I can't," answered Susie, in tones that sounded very clear, loud, and firm beside his.

" But you must."

Still Susie showed all the reluctance to answer that a newly caged wild bird does to sing.

Hungerford hardly knew what he had expected from her when she should first be placed in the position of the claimed, but of her final answer he had almost made himself certain.

" Listen," said Susie, twirling herself round on the music-seat, " I have been making a little plan in my head in this last minute ; this is it. I'll blindfold you with my pocket-handkerchief, and lead you to

quite the other end of the room, and twist
you round three times; then you must find
your way to the piano, and strike one note
at random with one finger. If the note is
C my answer shall be si, yes. If you strike
any other note, why, then——" Her
sentence trailed off into uncertainty.

" What a childish proposition !" he said,
half angry, half amused.

" But it seems to suit me so well," said
Susie, in a propitiating tone.

"You are right, it does. Having set my
preference on a child, I must take the con-
sequences. So blindfold me."

He dropped on his knees beside her.
Susie drew a small gossamer handkerchief
from her pocket.

" Too small," she said, trying to knot it
at the back of his dark, haughty head :
" you must give me your own."

He gave it to her, and she fastened it
securely over his eyes ; then she sat looking
at his half-hidden profile, silent and embar-
rassed.

" Now," he said, gropingly putting
forth one hand, " now for the rest of it. I
am to be led to the further end of the room,
turned round three times, and left to find
my bewildered way to the piano to strike
the note C !'

" Perhaps you may strike it, perhaps
not," said she, hastily. " There are six of
them besides C. You may chance on
another, since there are six !"

" It shall be perfectly fair," said Ranicar,
laughing easily. " Come, lead me away."

Susie, limply taking the ends of his
fingers, led him across the room to the
space in the bow-window opposite the
piano. The rain was beating angrily

15—2

against the panes ; people hurried past,
their heads bent slavishly to the wind. In
an opposite window a child was being
dragged away with its mouth wide open
as if screaming. She turned Hungerford
round three times.

" Now, how many fingers do I hold up ?"
she asked, with implicit, childlike confidence
in his good faith.

" One," said Ranicar unhesitatingly.

" Go," was her answer ; " I am holding
up two, so you cannot see."

Ranicar walked gropingly across the room
to settle his fate. He found the piano ;
Susie, on tip-toe, followed him noiselessly, and with craning neck, parted lips,
wide-open eyes, and clasped hands watched
his uplifted finger slowly descending on
the key-board. The thoughts flitting
through her mind were a confusion of

childishness and worldly wisdom ; but it was with a deep breath almost amounting to a sob, that she saw the long slender finger with its filbert nail come down with a crash on the note C. Ranicar with his other hand tore off the handkerchief.

" Mine !" he said, turning and catching her in his arms. "Say, yes, with your own sweet lips, Susie ; or I will be satisfied if you say si."

" You could see ;" was the way Susie obeyed him ; she spoke with a heartfelt resentment.

He laughed.

" I could not."

" *Please* let me go !"

" No."

And for the first time in her seventeen years, Susie was given the unpeaceful kiss of love.

"I have a happiness that I can grasp!" exclaimed Hungerford, still not releasing her. His voice had a ring in it of the youth he had lost.

"Happiness," said Susie, and in her tones was all the melancholy of a blurred future. "What is happiness?"

"This," he answered, again pressing his lips on hers. "To me," he added, looking her in the face.

At this moment footsteps were heard approaching the door. Susie started, and Ranicar released his hold on her.

"Mr. Everard," announced the servant, and Susie, looking like a culprit caught in flagrant misdemeanour, murmured half a greeting to Eugene, did not hold out her hand, was filled with the most gnawing confusion and embarrassment. Ranicar, of course, was just as usual, but his heart was

full of maledictions against the dangerous
intruder who had come to pay an afternoon
call. Any slight awkwardness that there
may have been in the situation was quickly
put an end to by Mrs. Willis coming into
the room.

Eugene being an excellent manœuvrer,
it was only a few minutes before he was at
the piano turning over the sheets of some
new songs with Susie, while Ranicar was
left to chafe inwardly as he talked com-
monplaces with Mrs. Willis. Mrs. Willis
felt vaguely regretful that she had not
given directions to have any visitor who
might come, shown into another room. It
was a large house, and there were three *en
suite.*

" Why did you look so guilty and at a
loss when I came in ?" asked Eugene of
Susie, wishing to force from her a reply to

the question that he had already answered
in his own mind.

" Because I felt so."

"Then I must ask you why you felt so?"

" No, you must not."

" But I shall, and do."

Susie was silent.

"Hungerford can give you everything in
the world," said Eugene quietly, finding
that she did not intend to reply. " To a
poor dependent dog like myself, he seems a
very enviable fellow, with his lot of money
and his mastery over his own actions. I
suppose I must congratulate you?"

Susie shook her head, purposely making
the motion as meaningless as she could.

Eugene watched her narrowly. To eyes
that daily studied the sense-pleasing beauty
of the Creole as his did, the passionless
purity, and faulty fascination of Susie's

small white face, were unsatisfying to his lower, stronger nature, while his higher, weaker nature felt the nameless charm as the blind feel and delight in the fresh wind blowing scents and sounds of unseen flowers and birds to them.

"I must let her slip away from me!" thought he, and sighed. "And if I have a little heart-ache to see her belonging to Hungerford, Léontine shall console me. I'll congratulate *him*, of course," he said. "How very rustic of me not to have said that *first*. I called this afternoon to ask your aunt if she was going to have a séance to-night. She usually has one on Tuesdays."

"If she has one at all—and I have heard nothing about it—she will not have Mr. Van Vleck and his niece for the performers," said Susie, with a faltering coldness. "You

had better go to my aunt yourself and ask
her," she continued, rising and moving away
to where Mrs. Willis and Hungerford were.

There was a numb feeling about her
heart, and an aching sensation in her throat
which only a fit of weeping could have relieved. Naturally her pride and self-control drove back the tears, but sent these
painful sensations to take their place.

She found herself counting the lapis-
lazuli balls in Hungerford's watch chain,
while she listened to Eugene asking her
aunt, and pronouncing the Creole's name.

She heard her aunt reply that there was
to be a séance in her house to-morrow
evening, with a new spiritualist light—

> "A wisp that flickered
> Where no foot could tread—"

a Miss Milly King. She heard Eugene's
conditional consent to come, then her cold

hand was grasped by his warm one in fare-well, and presently he was gone.

There had been but very few words ex-changed between them ; nothing had been said to mar the brightness of her fate, yet she felt it to be marred ; she felt herself a miserably free agent to dispose of her future as she chose. She dreaded being left alone with Hungerford again.

" I wonder," thought she, " if I make a sort of prayer to Aunt Adria not to go away, and look at her all the while, it will not show through my eyes, and force her to stay."

This was Susie's idea of animal magne-tism.

Mrs. Willis half got up, then sank back again. It was not of much importance, of course, that a being, who at the end of an uncertain number of years would find an affinity for her never-dying soul in the spirit land, should be left to arrange about taking a fleeting and wearisome pilgrimage with a fellow pilgrim—but—Mrs. Willis's soaring mind dropped down like a tired bird for a moment, and she remembered her own young love-dream, and the stolen interviews that had seemed to her so many prizes snatched from time, and infinitely more important than those spiritual prizes of progression, perfected will-power, psychical selection. She rose up, and left her niece alone with her lover, and the prayer in her heart that had proved ineffectual.

An hour later Susie was standing in her room before the glass, gazing at the reflection of her face.

"I think I must have underrated myself," she thought, with a complacency that she had never enjoyed before. "My eyes

are the colour of the sky, seen through old-
fashioned greenish glass windows, which
must be uncommon. My nose is unob-
trusive, which must be an advantage ; it
points heavenward, too, which is considered
a fine idea, as to the spire of a church. My
mouth is jolly when I am happy, and pretty
when I am sad, and the corners droop as
they do now. My skin is as examinable as
a quite new white kid glove. Bah !" she
concluded, turning away in disgust, " if I
were Miss Léontine Médor, I should be
looking at eyes like a stag's at bay, nose
that Helen or Cleopatra would not have
turned up their noses at. Oh, how delightful to have your own beauty staring
you in the face."

As she had not any beauty of her own to
stare her in the face, she dressed without
once again looking in the glass, and with

coils of hair very one-sided, and a crooked bow at her neck, went down to the drawing-room, where she found her aunt sitting alone reading.

Susie in faltering words told her that she was engaged to Mr. Hungerford.

" I am sure that your mother will quite approve," said Mrs. Willis, drawing her down and kissing her abstractedly somewhere near her ear. " Alice"—to her daughter, who, following the advice of Zeno, had trampled pain beneath her feet, and now made her appearance for the first time that day—" Alice, Susie has a piece of news for you."

" Have you ?" said Alice, turning on her cousin. " Engaged ! and to Mr. Hungerford, of course. I know it without your telling me. And you are very happy, of course ?"

" I suppose I feel as other girls do who
are called happy," said Susie.

" He is a great deal older than you,"
returned Alice. " What strange fancies
men do take !"

" Yes," said Susie, eagerly, and not at
all offended. " Another instance is Mr.
Everard and the medium, Miss Médor."

" Oh, do you think so ?" remarked Alice,
sceptically. " I do not call that an instance. He does not care for her."

" No ?" said Susie, breathlessly.

Alice held up her hand, screwed her
wrist round, bent her head down to meet
it, and, blushing, snapped a tight bracelet
together.

" No," she answered, with an air of sly
satisfaction. " From the way he has spoken
to me, I am positive that he—that it—oh,
I know exactly how it is. If he were to

go away to-morrow, he would forget her the day after to-morrow."

To transfer her jealousy from Léontine to Alice was not much of a consolation to Susie. That Eugene had said many gracious flattering nothings to her cousin she did not doubt. Well ! husks should be the food for vanity.

"Perhaps you think so," she said, as a reply to her cousin's last words. "I do not; she is so beautiful."

"But as dark as a mulatto, almost," exclaimed Alice, detractingly, and mentally reviewing her own blonde charms.

"So beautiful," repeated Susie, in heart-hungry tones. "He could not forget her face all at once."

"What sort of engagement ring shall you have?" asked Alice.

"I don't know," answered Susie, "why

should I have any? I think if I'm asked,
I'll say that I'll have a black pearl set in
black enamel."

"A mourning ring!" said Alice, sourly.
" Of course as a compliment to Mr. Hungerford, nothing could be more *apropos.*"

Susie only laughed.

" Come, come, children !" said Mrs.
Willis, with languid annoyance. "You
have made a very good match, Susie ; pray
do not forget to thank your guardian spirit
to-night."

" My guardian spirit ?" echoed Susie in
surprise. "I did not know I had one.
My thanks and my prayers are to God,
Aunt Adria."

" Oh, very well ; educate the soul by
probity, integrity, consideration for others,
and your prayers and thanks will no doubt
be acceptable. And magnanimity," said Mrs.

Willis, plunging back into the middle of her sentence again.

"Magnanimity," said Susie, slowly and carefully, as if afraid that she might forget some of the syllables. "That means the noblest sort of kindness?"

"Yes; magnanimity forgives quickly and ungrudgingly, not slowly and sparingly. It is cheerful charity, all-embracing faith, all-cherishing hope."

CHAPTER XV.

THE CHILDREN'S PARTY.

SUSIE was walking in Kensington Gardens with the children and their governess. Her betrothed had gone down to the Isle of Wight to see Mrs. Dawnay. Susie was not without a pleasurable sense of freedom, and stepped along with almost a jaunty air again, although there was a perplexed and discontented look in her face.

Eugene, strolling along one of the leafless

16—2

alleys towards twelve o'clock came up with
her, and paused by her side.

" You're not riding to-day ?" he said.

" No, I did not feel inclined to ride ;
Alice is riding without me."

" And how is Hungerford ?"

" I don't know ; he went down to Beaucome this morning to see mamma."

" Ha ! for the official seal, as it were.
Happy Hungerford !"

Susie, glancing at him, saw that he looked
haggard and restless, and not happy Everard
by any means. She wondered what trou-
bles were pressing on him, to give the restlessness of heart and mind and purpose
which was shown in his face.

As she was about to speak, the children,
rushing up panting from behind, caught
each an arm, and hung there, nestling themselves closely to their cousin with an air of

confidence and fearlessness of rebuke. She was not so lavish of the word "don't" as their sister.

"Do you enjoy walking with your cousin?" asked Eugene.

"Yes," answered Cora, a hazel-eyed, pale-faced, straight-featured child, with sharp, ever-working wits. "We like better to have Susie go with us than Alice; Alice always wants to go in the streets, and she is always looking at herself in the shop-windows; she pretends she is looking at the things; I know she isn't, because she looks into furniture-shops, iron-shops, seed-shops, empty shops, and all."

Eugene laughed; but the laugh, in spite of himself, ended in a tired yawn.

" I am blue," he said, apologetically.

"Suppose," returned Susie, looking at him with a half womanly, half childlike expression of compassion, "that you come to the party to-night—Lucy's birthday party that she is going to have. It might cheer you up, perhaps. I know that Aunt Adria would be delighted for you to think it worth while to come; and Lucy would be very *pwoud* to have you—wouldn't you, *r*-less one?" bending down and looking into the child's face.

Lucy only hung her head in confusion.

Eugene, whose evenings now for a long time had been spent in *amusing* himself at the Creole's, hesitated at the idea of disposing of his time elsewhere. But as a thirsty man may desire cold water rather than the rich wine drunk to the confusion of the faculties, the dulling of the perceptions, the fevering of the senses, so he was willing to exchange those fiery draughts of "amusement" for the insipid and pure refreshment of a few hours in the society of children—and Susie.

"I should like to come very much," he said gravely, casting down a glance at Lucy, "but you see I'm not invited."

"We are going to have a *ring* in the cake; we are going to dance; we are going to play games," said Lucy, lifting large, shy eyes, and setting forth the attractions of her natal day celebration.

"But you haven't asked *me* to play games, nor *me* to dance; and as for the cake, I don't believe you would let me have a slice to try my luck for the ring."

"Oh, yes!"

"You would? And if I get it, I promise to give it away to somebody. Who shall it be?"

"Me."

"Ah! now I shall come. At what time?"

"Five," said Susie; "five till nine. He cannot help trying to please even Lucy," she thought.

Gliding along one of the side-paths, stopping every now and then to read the Latin name at the foot of some tree or shrub, was to be seen a tall woman, in a dark, heavy dress. The figure had a pronounced individuality.

"I think I see some one that I must speak to," said Eugene, hurriedly, his mind taking a leap from careless playfulness to eager earnest. "Au revoir."

He moved away as abruptly as he spoke, and in a moment they saw him beside the woman, whose face had never been turned towards them. He walked slowly off, in a listening attitude. The back of the girl had been as easily recognizable by Susie as if she had stood face to face with her.

"What a tall lady!" remarked Cora. "I hope I shall be as tall as that when I finish growing. It will be fun having Mr. Everard to-night. Can he play games just like us, Susie?"

"Oh! he can play any sort of game," answered Susie, with a child's pout, a woman's bitterness. "Walk slower, children; we are leaving Miss Wix too far behind."

All shyness, and white muslin and coral beads, the little hostess gave her minute hand to her tall guest, with a blush of mingled fright and satisfaction.

Susie, seated at the piano, was holding a child on her lap, while she guided its fat fingers over the keys for an accompaniment to the baby voice shrilling out "Ten Little Niggers."

Bestowing a few words on Alice, which

increased the complacency of her expression, Eugene made his way over to Susie, and waited patiently for the diminution of the ten little niggers to one. Then the child, having wriggled down and run romping away, to add its mite to the ever-increasing Babel, Susie was at liberty to look up and attend to him. But he was very silent; and the air of unrest that he had worn in the morning was unchanged.

"I am going to play for them to dance; go and get a little partner," said she, coaxingly. "A *very* little one, for the sake of being funny; you are so tall."

"But not so tall as Hungerford, you know."

"He is extremely tall," answered Susie. "I think he has grown since I saw him first. Go, Mr. Everard, and take that little thing with a frock that has no belt."

" That baby?"

" She can dance."

" Do you know," said Everard, lowering his voice, " how *very much* I should like a dance with you ? Will not some one else play ?"

" Oh, yes, Miss Wix ; after she has seen about some things."

Eugene moved away, and Susie watched him bending himself double to meet the needs of his baby-curled partner's exceeding low stature. He had obediently taken the infant of her selection. She laughed heartily, and then she knew how sore-hearted she was ; for her laughter seemed to touch the source of her tears, instead of being the outcome of genuine amusement.

Afterwards Miss Wix took her place, and she danced indefatigably with the children, singling out always the plainly dressed and insignificant ones, whose little companions, with the snobbishness unfortunately discernible even in children, shirked them.

"Come," said Eugene, advancing towards her smiling, as she stood resting for a moment, " you ought to reward me by giving me a dance, for I really have been making myself an awfully entertaining fellow to the smallest of them in the next room; and to be thoroughly entertaining to human beings of that age I find one has to put up with a good deal of bodily discomfort, such as going on all fours till you feel apoplectic, and bumping your head against the brackets, playing blind man's buff, and the rest of it.   Come."

Susie hesitated a moment, but Miss Wix was playing such an enticing waltz, and Eugene danced thoroughly well.   She laid her hand on his shoulder, and they glided away.

As they paused for breath a tall figure strode in among the children, like Gulliver among the Lilliputians. It was Mr. Hungerford, just returned from the Isle of Wight. He looked eagerly about for Susie, and seeing her, bent his steps towards her.

"Back again!" cried she, springing forward to meet him. "Oh, how is mamma?"

"Quite well," he answered, drawing her arm through his, and leading her away. "What were you doing? Dancing with Everard?"

"Yes."

"You did not expect me to return so soon, perhaps?" he said in a tone of cold vexation.

"Don't you wish me to dance with him? I will not now that you have come." (He was disarmed.) "Oh do tell me about mamma.

How was she looking? Did not your heart go out to meet her? Didn't you wonder how she ever came to have such a daughter?"

" She is lovely, most lovely," he replied, warming with enthusiasm. " She ,, is everything that is charming, and graceful, and lovable. I have never seen any one more ——"

" And did she like you?" asked Susie, ruthlessly cutting him short, and throwing all the eagerness into her voice that was in her upraised eyes.

Ranicar smiled. " If there is any liking to be gained by an admiration so profound that it cannot help making itself evident, then really, I must be liked by Mrs. Dawnay."

" Did she like you *very much?*" continued Susie, intensifying her tone and glance.

"She must tell you that, not I. She did
not, naturally, measure out her opinion of
me in words and sentences that I can re-
peat to you."

There was something very unflattering
in these eager, bald inquiries. They proved
to a certainty that Susie had not pre-sup-
posed the value that her mother would set
on him as a son-in-law, or the impression
he would make on her.

"At least," added he, "I am able to tell
you that your mother confides you and
your happiness to my keeping."

"Well! I daresay it is all real," said
Susie, speaking and sighing together.
"But I somehow feel as if I were *playing*
at being engaged."

A lover's interpretation of a somewhat
doubtful speech was the one that Ranicar
gave to this.

" Here is something that will perhaps make it seem more real," he said in a low, tender voice, and slipping a ring on her finger. Susie looked at it as if it was a scar or disfigurement that an unfortunate accident had afflicted her hand with.

" Do you like it ? Perhaps I should have asked you to tell me what stone you preferred."

" This one is very beautiful," rejoined Susie, recovering herself, and looking more hospitably at the great diamond flashing on her finger. "It seems almost too handsome for me. I feel as if I had become the protector of something more. valuable than I am myself. I know now exactly what the sensations of the guardians of little Royalties are."

"Susie, Susie, your charming conversation is flavoured with the most childish nonsense."

"This is a children's party," said Susie, the word "childish" being a suggestive one. "Come, you must help entertain the children; you must dance, you must be amusing."

"Entertain the children?—dance?" he repeated, and the melancholy of his eyes, the haughty carriage of his whole tall form, seemed to make her words unsuitable and incongruous. " I never dance now."

"No!" said Susie, looking at him with the greatest astonishment. "And you must know how so perfectly."

"Do you think that an ultra-civilized human being should take the same delight in dancing that a savage does?"

"Why I am just as civilized as you are," returned Susie, combatively, "and yet I *love* dancing."

"You are seventeen, and dancing is always among the loves of civilized seventeen. I daresay the taste of an ice gives you a pleasurable emotion, and the sight of a box of bon-bons would make you blush with satisfaction as few satisfactions will be able to make you blush when you are seven and thirty."

"I don't know about all that," said Susie doubtfully, "but I know that I love dancing. And if you can't dance, you can play games; so come and play. You must indeed help to amuse these little girls and boys. Miss Wix must play for the older ones to dance, Aunt Adria is arranging the things for the lottery, and Alice is doing what she can."

"Yes," said Ranicar, moving to where he could obtain a view of the adjoining room, "at this moment she is opening and shutting her fan, and talking to Everard with a sort of perturbed coquetry."

"Come," said Susie, becoming more eager

and impatient to play games, and running out of the little room at the end of the suite—into which he had taken her, because they had it to themselves—into the next, where the juvenile sports of flirtation and hunt the slipper were going on (the flirtation was limited to Alice and Eugene).

The children were tired of hunt the slipper, and Lucy ran up to her cousin, demanding, as she came, a nice new game.

"Let me think," said Susie, giving all her mind to it, in a way that delighted Ranicar, "what have you played?"

Two or three little voices clamoured the names of the played-out games.

"We'll have Stage Coach," said Susie, decidedly, "and you, Mr. Hungerford, shall tell the story. Now mind you make it very funny, so that they will be convulsed with laughter" (this in his ear), "for Lucy wants them to go away, and say that it is the nicest party they have ever been at in their lives."

" My dear Susie, I could not make a child laugh."

" *A* child laugh ! Why I expect you to make them all laugh, every one of them."

" Impossible. Tell the story yourself."

" No, they would not be half so well satisfied with me. I cannot help but think it disobliging of you. Well ! if you will not, I must ask Mr. Everard. He has done already everything most kind. He has been blindfolded while his hand was painted to look like a face (he pretending all the time that he did not know the trick of it), and a crying doll's cap put on it, and a long doll's dress over his arm. He has played blind man's buff (letting himself be caught over and over again) ; he has danced with the smallest scraps of children just because I asked him—I shall go to him and tell him I want him for Stage Coach."

" I am quite willing to be outdone by him, and to admit that he has the power of adapting himself to children of the tenderest age, while I am deficient ; but I object to your interrupting his conversation with your cousin to ask him. I will tell the story. Just start me please, and give me a few heads or leading points."

" Sit down, children, and name yourselves," said Susie.

Then began a scramble for seats; marked preferences and avoidances being shown with an honesty cloaked in riper years, and there was an overpowering chorus of treble voices, crying out, "I'll be the door," —" I'll be the baby,"—" I'll be —" this, that, and the other.

"Now," said Susie, indicating to Hungerford a conspicuous chair in the centre of
the attentive circle, "now, you know, of
course, that you must begin by saying,
'Once upon a time a Stage Coach was
going down hill —' and after that the only
thing to do is to"—here came an interruption in the shape of Alice and Eugene
joining the circle, and having to have names
provided for them—"is to tell as funny a
story as you can think of, bringing in all
those words as often and as drolly as you
possibly can."

"Very well," said Ranicar. "Once upon
a time a Stage Coach was going downhill—
say on the Corniche Road."

Eugene looked swiftly away from Susie,
to whom he had begun talking, to the
obliteration of the child between himself
and her.

" 'There were in this coach an old (or young) maid ;"—(old maid gets up, twirls itself like a teetotum, and subsides)—" a crying baby, two or three more passengers, a hamper —." Here he enumerated the imaginary contents of the coach, stringing together a strange and subtle story; which, if it did not *amuse* the children, caused them to sit open-mouthed, straining their little wits with an interest that made them forget to twirl their small selves when their name was mentioned.

The subtlety of the story lay in its having interwoven with it facts pregnant with distressful meaning to one mind present.

Eugene, bound by conventional fetters to sit still and listen, clenched his teeth so hard that the joint of the jaw ached up into his temple. It was almost unendurable that he should thus have recalled to him the only time in his life when he had suffered acutely, when he had had forced to his lips a draught of self-contempt "bitterer to drink than blood." It was so *rusé* on the part of Hungerford. It was like finding an infernal machine in a child's toy. He fixed his eyes resolutely on Ranicar's neck-tie, to convey the impression that he was looking him in the face, which in reality he was unable to do. For an instant he looked away, glancing sideways at Susie, and Susie's two grey eyes met his with an expression of wondering perplexity, for Susie had very quick perceptions, and though she did not in the least understand the tragic under-current of that child's game, she was confounded by a look in the faces of both men, who were making the trivial play a medium for the expression of most virile animosity.

Eugene had never known before, that the brother of the young and high-strung girl who had not been able to bear a defeated love, saw in him the destroyer of his sister's happiness; and that he should select so strange a place and manner for making him aware of his knowledge, filled him with mortification, and angry wonder, and desire of retaliation. He knew that it was the expression of his own face that had committed him to Susie, and he felt an active resentment against the man who had arrayed masked enemies of words before him to stab him in the dark, and force his own lips and eyes to betray him.

Ranicar's story drew to a close. There was a finale of laughter and romping and confusion, and the game of Stage-Coach was over.

"Did I do it well?" asked Ranicar of Susie.

"No," she answered, frankly; "the children did not understand you. You were making it serve some purpose of your own, which I could not, of course, fathom, but I think Mr. Everard did; perhaps you meant him to."

"You are remarkably keen-sighted. He is a double-hearted fellow, Susie." The last words were as the whirling straws that betray the vortex.

"I had rather you did not tell me so, even if it is your honest opinion of him," she said, moving away.

He strode after her, and in his icy tone of displeasure, more formidable than the out-blazing of anger, said, "Why do you shrink from hearing me tell you in confidence what I know Everard to be?"

"Because," answered she, her hands growing cold and tremulous, her voice unsteady, "because he has something so winning, so *promising* in his face——"

"*Promising!*" repeated Ranicar, with angry contemptuousness; "no doubt; promising that which no woman ever finds fulfilled. He is a man who is taken on trust because his face and his smooth tongue belie him. He is a man who makes his own life enjoyable by defrauding others of their capacity for enjoyment. You will never hear me speak in this way of any other fellow man, therefore give me your belief; and give me your obedience too, for I am going to demand a promise from you that in future you make a complete stranger of Everard; that there is to be no dancing with him; no riding, no walking in Kensington Gardens. Your cousin tells me that this morning you were walking there with him, and that it was you who asked him to come here to-night. Why did you ask him? Is his society so very agreeable, so *precious* to you?"

Susie's heart of hearts answered "Yes." Susie's hitherto truthful tongue faltered out "N-no, but she had always liked Mr. Everard."

"You are a child, and charitably childish in your construction of things. Now give me your word that from to-night you make of Everard a stranger, who is to cross your path as little as he crosses mine."

"Very well," said Susie, in a low tone, "I will copy your way of treating him as exactly as I can; that will be most satisfactory to you, of course."

There was something in her way of speaking not at all satisfactory to him:

He looked down at her with an air of angry surprise.

" That is a singular way of answering," he said. " I have never heard you speak in that tone and manner before."

" Because I have never been asked before to give such a promise," replied Susie, with something like retort. " How you dislike Mr. Everard !"

" If you saw his character as I see it, you would understand that my dislike for him was one of my claims to hatred of falsity."

" You are robbing him of every claim to be liked."

" If there was any danger of your liking him, I am glad that I am. Still another thing, and then we will have done with speaking of him. He is weak enough to be always determined that his liking and ad-miration for a woman shall be justified by having that woman the object of some other man's preference. Where a selection has been made by some one whose opinion he values, he too selects, with a view to supplanting. He has never been known to have any originality of choice until now."

"Until now ?" repeated Susie, questioningly, and lifting up a face that had grown crimson because of the sting contained in his words.

"Yes ; until now. I have not heard of any one but himself throwing away their emotions on that weird and fiery creature, the American Medium." He had spoken throughout to his young love as one having authority ; but Susie, who would have accepted with meekness his dictum on other less significant matters, chose to cleave still to her simple belief in Eugene's clear blue eyes and unclouded features, his life-loving smile and sympathetic voice.

" I thought him very nice the first time I saw him, and I should not be surprised if I always thought him so," she returned, with innocent, inoffensive persistence.

" Very well ; I have placed him before you in his true light. Keep to your own childish and superficial judgment, if you please, but maintain a consistent coldness towards him, remember, for he is a man whom you *must not* have for a friend. Some day, when you are dearer and closer to me even than now, I will sadden that young heart of yours by telling you a story of which he is the contemptible—hero. Not now, not now. I see your lips parting inquisitively. Would you like me to dance one dance with you ? You think I must know how perfectly—"

"I am tired," said Susie, shrinking away from the arm that would have encircled her, "and you have not told me half of what there must be to tell about mamma."

Here hands small but rough clutched her; voices all shrill, and trying to out-speak one another, clamoured for her; she was hurried away into the next room, blind-folded, and imprisoned within a circle of small figures, a walking-stick in her hand; she was a child playing with children, and Ranicar—a lonely man, whom the world had tired—was left standing among the little dancers (who sometimes stumbled against him and jostled him), looking over their heads at the wand-like figure of his love, surrounded by a restless ring of children.

CHAPTER XVI.

A MORNING WALK.

"BUT I have come expressly to walk with you."

"Then you must go away expressly *not* to walk with me."

"Why?"

"Because—"

The children's party was an affair of only last night. It was the early hour of 10 a.m., and Ranicar, to whom breakfast at nine and a walk afterwards·did not come within the range of possibility, was at the moment asleep and dreaming. But Eugene was broad awake and acting.

"'Because you are engaged' is the way to end the sentence," I suppose ; "but I don't find your engagement an argument against my walking down this quiet alley with you, a governess behind, two children in front. I like watching children run races."

"There are plenty of other children to watch."

"True," he answered, looking full at her, "but I like, too, watching something else of which there is but one in the world."

"It is always a pleasure to me to do any little thing I can for people," said Susie, completely putting aside his last words. "Wait, children. As you are so fond of seeing races run, I'll gratify you by running one, to run away from you. One, two, three, and away! See if you can catch me, Cora."

She ran off; a word or two of expostulation reaching her from Miss Wix.

She was caught up with, but not by Cora. Cora was seen coming panting towards them, well distanced.

"I can be quite as young and frisky as you are," said Eugene.

Susie looked very self-condemned as he spoke, and, turning away from him, transformed herself from a child to a woman, walking with measured steps to meet Miss Wix, with whom she came gravely back.

"I think," said little Miss Wix, with a sense of what was becoming, "that we will take a shorter walk than usual this morning, as you were very tired last night. Come, Miss Cora, we are going to turn off here."

Eugene—whom to baffle was to energize —felt himself dismissed. He said good-morning with a bright smile, and walked away to Swanbury Crescent.

"Mamma," said Alice, just before luncheon, bursting into her mother's dressing-room, with an Italian book under her arm, "Susie ought not to be meeting Mr. Everard in Kensington Gardens when she is walking with Miss Wix and the children, ought she?"

Mrs. Willis turned her ground-glass eyes with their dilated pupils on her daughter— she was reading "Hesperia," and the interruption came to her as a sudden glare of daylight upon a man groping underground by lantern-light for treasure.

"Does she meet him?" said she, trying to concentrate her faculties on the unimportant present of her niece.

" She meets him constantly. Cora told me just now that she had met him this morning. It is very wrong to Mr. Hungerford, isn't it? He ought to be told, I think. Shall not you tell him, mamma?"

" No," said Mrs. Willis, waving her hand impatiently, " her mother will be in town before long, and I shall be able to free myself of the responsibility of Susie. Your Aunt Margaret will manage these things for her, and see that Mr. Hungerford is not improperly treated; but I will say a word to Susie about it."

" And you shall not tell Mr. Hungerford?"

" No. Go down, Alice, and tell Susie to come up here to me. Don't come back yourself, and shut the door gently."

" Do you want me, Aunt Adria?" came in Susie's young voice.

"Yes," replied Mrs. Willis, closing her book on one finger; "sit down. I merely wish to say to you that I disapprove of Mr. Everard joining you in your early walks with the children. I hear that he is in the habit of meeting you——"

"Oh, no!" cried Susie, "only sometimes. I tried this morning to appear annoyed. I think he saw it. I believe it will prevent his coming again."

"You had better give up your walks in the morning if there is danger of your meeting him." Mrs. Willis withdrew her finger from the leaves of her book. "I hope," she said, "that you have not entered too lightly on your engagement. That you questioned your real self—your soul—before you gave your promise to him. It is only for earth-life, certainly, that you have agreed to be his; but it is a probationary stage, this earth-life, and we must not trail the wings of our divine indweller, the soul, in the dust of unjust, underhand, or pusillanimous actions. Where is the beautiful ring that you showed me last night? Why is it not where he placed it, my dear?"

She had taken Susie's left hand in hers, and was looking into her niece's face with some warmth of interest.

"It is so *terribly* handsome and valuable," murmured Susie, blushing. "I am going to put it on when I dress for dinner."

"But Mr. Hungerford is to lunch here; he will be here now at any moment. What will he think to see that you have taken off the *gage d'amour* he has just given you?"

As she spoke these words, Susie comprehended for the first time what her aunt must have been like in the young days when she disobeyed her parents and married Mr. Willis.

"I'll go and put it on," she answered, indifferently, and at this moment the sound of the knocker was heard.

"Lucy," said Alice, who was in the school-room with her sisters, a room behind the dining-room, from whose door the front hall was visible, "peep out and see if that is Mr. Hungerford. Cora," she continued when the little one's back was turned, "Susie and I want you to tell Mr. Hungerford that Mr. Everard was walking with you in Kensington Gardens this morning again."

"He was running races with us," amended Cora.

"Very well, tell him that. Don't forget, and I'll give you that little tatting-case of mine, which looks like a porte-monnaie."

" Will you ? Indeed, then I shan't forget Ally, I'll tell him the minute I see him."

Alice made no reply ; hurrying from the room upstairs to her own.

Hardly were they seated at the luncheon table, before Cora, in a round, clear voice, burst out :—

" Mr. Everard was running races with us this morning in Kensington Gardens, Mr. Hungerford."

" Was he ? With you and your little sister ?"

" Yes ; with Lucy and Susie and me."

" Ah !" said Ranicar, unmoved. " And who won ?"

" Oh ! Susie and Mr. Everard. I shouldn't have been so far behind if Lucy hadn't tumbled down, and I stopped to pick her up. I wish I hadn't."

Ranicar, with admirable self-control, cast not a glance at Susie, and refrained from the faintest show of annoyance. Only seeming to think that speaking of running races in the early morning led up to the subject of early rising and its effects on character and constitution.

Susie listened with an unburthened conscience for which her lover did not give credit, joining in the conversation gaily.

Poor child! Although she would not admit it to herself, the very fact of Eugene's caring to seek her, caring to walk with her, choosing to tell her that there was only one face like hers in the world, and that it pleased him to watch it, eased her heart of its secret trouble, leaving only a vague misgiving to torment her still.

After luncheon the Willis family dispersed this way and that like rays of the rising sun. Only Susie and Ranicar were left in the drawing-room.

Susie sat on the arm of a large chair whose cushion was occupied by Charlie. She was drawing his long silken ears through her fingers ; Ranicar's ring flashed on one of them.

" Susie," Hungerford began at once, " is this the way that you yield to my wishes, and carry out your own words in which I put my trust ?"

" You mean about Mr. Everard I suppose," said Susie, bluntly. She disdained the shallow evasion of pretended misunderstanding. "I was rather sorry to see him," she continued, "and I told him to go. Then I ran a race with the children, not for him to run too, but to run away from him."

" I wish," said Hungerford, frowning, " that I could share these early walks with you; but I am a very poor sleeper, and the morning hours are the only ones I cannot spare to you out of my whole day. But if Everard has the bad taste ever again to force his presence on you, you are to give them up. I prohibit them."

"Oh, but the children will be so miserable! Why, they will hardly go now without me."

"Nonsense. You understand you are to give them up. Susie," he went on, clasping the hand and the spaniel's ears that it would not relinquish, "you would have told me voluntarily that you had seen Everard this morning, would you not?"

"No," said Susie, with the utmost decision; "I should not really. I was so afraid that you might be angry, and I cannot bear to be scolded for what is not a bit my fault."

" Have I scolded you, my little love ?"

"No," answered Susie; "you have spoken quietly enough to me, but why should you not ? I have done nothing."

He pushed away the little dog, and seating himself in its place, clasped Susie, looking tenderly up into her face. She very coldly and shyly looked on the ground, and swayed away from him as far as possible.

" Oh !" she exclaimed, breaking the silence suddenly, while her expression grew bright and animated, " Mamma is coming up sooner than she intended. She will be here a week from yesterday ; Aunt Adria has got her rooms in Clarges Street, and I am going to her. I *am* so glad ! Aunt Adria is very kind indeed, but she seems to have taken a vow not to care for the trivial things of every-day life; and we all— I mean Uncle Willis and Alice and I and the children—come under that head. I suppose she is progressing, but every day we go back a little bit. Every day Cora gets more pert, and Lucy more shy and fonder of jam, and a greater cry-baby. And Uncle Willis is more and more in the city, and Miss Wix and the servants get more careless, and Alice grows vainer; and as for me, I do exactly what I please, and nobody seems to notice."

" But *I* shall see that you 'please' to do nothing against my wishes, so I am satisfied." After this there were things said which were as gall to her, as honey to him.

Her air of being on the defensive amused him; her small repulses he thought piquant; he found a delicious coyness in what was really a cold avoidance of his caresses. The averted cheek, the lowered eyelid, the half-frowning eyebrow, allured him more than all frank assurances of love given in tender glance, in soft smile, in head inclined towards him, would have done. These were not unknown to him.

There is nothing more blind than a satiated man of the world when he wooes a very young girl, who, proud of her conquest, and self-pleased with her great achievement, is loth to relinquish that which stings her small grasp.

There is strength in the very laxity of her half-willing hold. Nothing fetters a man so securely to a woman as a sense of freedom from bondage; and this sense he must have if she is perfectly unexacting; if she demands no time, no promises, no assurances, no confessions, no confidences, no sacrifices; and none of these things did Susie demand. Taking whatever her lover chose to give her with a calm acquiescence that had nothing of expectancy in it, nothing of the jealous exaction, the ever claiming appetite of vanity that Hungerford had always considered would be a tax on his slender stock of tolerance and patience.

"Are you happy?" he asked suddenly, touching the thick plaits of her hair.

"Oh, I am perfectly satisfied," she answered with a smile, but turning her eyes away from him and fixing them on the toe of a little velvet slipper thrust out prepense to serve her eyes.

He thought her manner at this moment full of quaint coquetry, and looked admiringly at the fascinating grace of her position and bend of the head.

"Why don't you say 'perfectly happy, Ranicar;' you have never called me by my name."

" I could not ; it is such a very unusual one. I don't like unusual names—in books."

"Come," he said with rather a vexed laugh, "That 'in books' was an after thought. You meant that you did not like unusual names simply. Call me Car then ; my sister used to call me that."

" It is short and easy to say, certainly," murmured Susie. "I will say it over aloud to myself when I am alone, and then perhaps I shall learn to call you so. Get down, Charles, you are in the way."

" This is your cousin's dog, is it not ?"

"Yes ; Mr. Everard gave it to her, and I was with him when he got it ; I did not know it at the time though."

" When and where was that ?" asked Hungerford, involuntarily letting the lids fall over his eyes until their burning light was concentrated to two fiery sparks.

" Down at Beaucome. We had been lunching with his uncle, and after luncheon I went for a drive with him."

" Alone ?"

" Yes. Mamma told him to be sure and not let me get out and scratch my hands and tear my frock, I remember ;" with a low laugh.

" Then you knew him very well down in Beaucome ?"

" No, I had not time ; he was only there two days."

" Susie, why does this speaking of Everard affect the circulation of your blood ? A moment ago you were pale, and now you are the colour of your coral beads."

His voice was quite low and even, but some influence in it, or in the guarded anger of his face made Susie regret her gratuitous frankness.

"If I am flushed," she answered, "it is because fire *will* scorch; I am sitting too near it. Let me move, please."

"And you were not going to tell me that he walked with you this morning? or did I misunderstand you? I hope I misunderstood you; it would not have been like your usual honesty (one of your chief charms to me) not to have told me."

"You did not misunderstand me. I was not going to tell you; I explained to you why."

"Perhaps," said Ranicar, looking at her less unfavourably, "in your admission that you did not intend telling me, there should be enough candour to satisfy me."

She did not answer, and again his face darkened as he watched her.

Alice, in her mischievous, malicious play, had done much to hasten the coming of the "little rift within the lute."

"Susie," said Hungerford, abruptly, "I think you understand that I am not a subject for even the most innocent coquetries to be practised on."

"No," she replied with some spirit, "I understand you hardly at all. You are so much beyond me in age and wisdom and cleverness, that I cannot know what you wish me to say and do, unless you tell me in so many words." When she reached the end of her speech the spirited tone had died away into one of the meekest conciliation.

"You know my wishes about Everard," he answered; "and though you tell me in such an ingratiating way that you will order your actions by my words, yet I know that you are too self-willed to submit to much dictation even from me. There, do not pout and frown, becoming as it is to you. Come to the piano, and sing me one song before I go. I have an engagement at five."

* * * * *

When Alice Willis went to her room that night, she saw a document of imposing dimensions pinned on her pincushion. She opened it, and found within the blank page of a copy-book, which was its enclosure, another torn-out page of a copy-book embellished with angular letters of monstrous size forming this excellent maxim : " Procrastination is the thief of time." Under it came in the same angular letters a trifle smaller :

"MY DEAR ALICE,

　　"Do not forget to give me the tatting-case.

　　　　"Your affectionate sister,

　　　"CORA LE MARCHANT WILLIS."

END OF VOL. I.

BILLING AND SONS, PRINTERS, GUILDFORD, SURREY.

www.ingramcontent.com/pod-product-compliance
Lightning Source LLC
Chambersburg PA
CBHW060559030726
47498CB00005B/1455